the last Orchard in america

by Michael Peck

THE2NDHAND | Nashville, Tenn. | the2ndhand.com
ISBN-10: 098346586X
ISBN-13: 978-0-9834658-6-7
Library of Congress Control Number: 2014943382

Cover and interior illustrations by Vinson Milligan

Combining the black-hearted noir of our haunted country with more twists and turns than anyone could predict. Better yet, in its narrator, Harry Jome, *Last Orchard* unleashes a voice as wry, surprising and inventive as any in recent memory.

> —**Peter Rock**, author of *The Shelter Cycle* and *My Abandonment*

A classical story of the damaged damsel limping alongside the recovering rogue toward parts unknown. And while it's clearly a novel that takes itself seriously, that doesn't mean the reader is never given a moment of levity, a break from the grim nature of the subject matter: "Anybody who gets his head knocked off by a slow-moving train is challenged in some special way." It's the beautiful bastard child of *The Long Goodbye*, *Pulp*, and *Confederacy of Dunces*.

> —**Andrew Armacost**, author of *The Poor Man's Guide to Suicide*

You know the guy: private gumshoe, buying his pistol back from hock, waiting on a tailor to finish his suit cuffs. You know the city, though here it helps that our hero has the eye of an architecture critic, pacing around the brutalist office blocks, monuments to extortionist drunks. Here daylight comes like "a premature baby…dangled in the trash-filled crevasses…wax[ing] gray and forbidding." And, yes, you know the genre, but this is noir on noir, cynical to the point of meta-reflection. "Real stories don't have morals or plots," our protagonist muses, and real mysteries are just that, jagged-edged puzzle pieces for which, at best, solution is an act of will and denial. After the dame has made her entrance, dripping sex, then gone like "curdled milk on an expensive porcelain saucer" and pulled out her blades and made her exit, all too fast, there's nothing left but a motel room that smells of death and more liquor on top of the liquor that has already stopped having any kind of effect. The dick picks up the Bible, that "first, monstrous piece of detective fiction," and a con plot, at that. Peck gives us a world "as wholesome as lice," in a tone that's as infectious, inescapable. You'll be itching through these pages for days after you're done, thinking back on the images of bridges or lines like this, about death: "Dying is just the fear of dying. I savored and chewed my breath as though it were poisoned oatmeal."

> —**Spencer Dew**, author of *Songs of Insurgency*, among others

Here's a book that any avid *Law & Order* or Dashiell Hammett fan—like my old lady—can get behind: a novel that's hilariously deadpan noir parody and excellent noir at the same time. It's like ruddy, half-polished wingtips in the rain, or like a simile.

> —**Jamie Iredell**, author of *The Book of Freaks*

ACKNOWLEDGEMENTS

To Todd Dills, who first published the short story that would become the serialization that would become this book, the kind of editor who allows writers to sleep easy. To Vinson Milligan for visualizing Harry Jome's world with meticulous care and artistry. To Paul "Bob" Varkusa, whose influence and hardboiled aesthetics pervade these pages. To Jeri Rafter—collaborator, early reader, superstar. To the editors who have helped my style in myriad ways. To my father and mother, whose faith in me has been unwavering. Finally, to my wife, a constant fount of love, inspiration, support and knowledge.

For Allison, always

The Last Orchard
in America

"Let us practice every imaginable grimace."
—Arthur Rimbaud

Let me begin before everything got all cockeyed and deadly and confused. Before Sue Longtree and Daddy Longtree and the orchard and Cowper and that bridge out of this despicable city. I blame a lot of this on my tailor, on that suave suit I was promised.

But I suppose if I wanted to go back before any of this I'd end up starting just after the dinosaurs were hacked to death by the wind and the earth and rotted away into fuel and dirt.

And where do you begin a story, anyway? Do you select some random point, or is there a tangible place that can be flipped over and pinpointed? "This is where everything started," you'd like to say. But any moment is a random accumulation of identical moments. There's not a definite beginning to anything. There can't be a beginning when everything is at an end.

I'm not a writer. I'm something more like a transcriber of degeneracy and hatred. Had I any poetic talents I would be talking about something better: Birds in migration, the pleasantries of intoxicated guests at a cottage on the Cape, beautiful women having a picnic on a rooftop, flowers peeling back to let in the morning.

Instead, I'm talking about rotting dinosaurs and the wretched people who have built this city with their capricious greed and cynicism.

I should say that nothing about this makes any kind of sense: there's no solution, I don't really know who's responsible, whether anything criminal has been committed by others, what my involvement in the Longtree situation really consisted of, or even if it consisted of anything other than a psychotic redhead's unquenchable love of her own self. And what I remember about Sue Longtree: the wave of that red hair, a smile that had in parted lips a riddle with no punchline, a scent, a stupid hope, a hand grasping my arm at a symphony performance.

"Why'd you do it, Jome?" Cowper says from across the

bridge.

I say, "I guess haven't slept too well lately."

And that should have been enough but it wasn't and it isn't.

The river is down below like a dark, wavering sheet and the men are closing in for the big squeeze, Cowper leading them, his face a featureless blank in relief against the massive spotlight behind him. I swing a leg over the metal railing, and then the other leg, balancing on the parapet like some mad acrobatic fool. The men's hard-bottomed shoes pound the concrete behind me and they're breathing heavy and I can almost feel their arms pulling me back.

It's funny, but the water below is so flat it looks like I could bounce right off the surface and carom back onto the bridge and find it empty of these animals in uniforms, replaced by daylight and a view of the city that hasn't been erased by the rain. And maybe that's exactly what I will do, when I am ready.

The river is getting closer, its contours in the night like an approximation of what I imagine the afterlife to be: black, trembling and not nearly deep enough. I put a foot out and my shoe drops off. I don't hear it plop into the river.

"Hey," Cowper yells. "Don't do that."

So where do I begin when there's nowhere to begin?

The morning I found Sue Longtree in my office I'd spent listening to a record of the adagio from a Mozart piano concerto, and I'd thought to myself that it was the simplest interpretation of innocence I'd ever pried out of the world. That sound—a soft piano fading—would be a halfway decent beginning, except that I've forgotten the tune it belonged to.

But anywhere, anybody is at least a halfway good beginning, if such a thing exists.

I **was at the window** looking out over the intersecting bridges spanning the city. Great hulking sculptures of metal and steel, able to withstand the fleeing and the returning with equal ease, layered on top of one another like a crazy staircase. Bridges are the strangest of modern conveniences, a street with no land underneath, a nowhere boulevard that can carry you across seas and lakes and rivers, transporting you to the elsewhere you yearn so vaguely to be. A bridge is neither the beginning nor the end of any journey.

The river beneath the webwork of bridges was sleek and consoling in its dangerous malaise, condemned to thrash, like all good rivers, against the encroachment of civilization.

A drop of rain struck the glass and eased down reluctantly. A siren careened three stories below in the street for a while, found its miserable destination and became a loose, fragile memory among a thousand others that one soon forgets. Then another siren joined in from somewhere beyond the first and the duet spun off to opposite fringes of the city, a cacophony of parting goodbyes in a town that is built of them.

It had been raining for weeks and the buildings out the window were becoming coated in a slick mirror of water that reflected the faded sky. I studied a calendar on my desk, trying to intuit what day it was, but the calendar was from last year and I'd never been keen on math. I sat back in my chair and grimaced at the ceiling.

I yawned, trying to surprise myself.

There was a blue and white marble on my desk that I began to roll back and forth on the uncluttered surface. The ninth or tenth time I was too slow and it bounced against a copy of a dog-eared Dominic Early novel that I'd been meaning to read. The marble dribbled onto the floor like any other sad, useless thing. I peered closely at the little round speck dreamily, urging it to keep rolling, but my momentary optimism wouldn't take. I left myself alone.

Sitting in the same position for hours, romanticizing the days you wasted in the gutter, you tend to disremember that the street exists, that there is something beyond the flickering wall clock in the berserk simplicity of a familiar room. That maybe you're a self-propelling organism with the nerve to feel all right; your body an urban development project and the brain a ticket-window to a carnival that is always vacant, though some silly bastard keeps the hallucinatory rides well oiled and moving along.

Lousiness doesn't achieve much more in one day.

That morning a middle-aged woman visited my office and offered me $400 to investigate the death of her husband. She was a babbling matron with the physique of a sack and lips purpled by wine, barely able to subvert a speech defect that slurred her words. The husband was decapitated by a train as he attempted to switch the tracks at some remote outpost beyond the suburbs. I tuned out what she was saying for a couple minutes, her mouth jabbering, until she noticed me not listening, and raised her voice.

"It was mysterious," the woman said. "In a week he was going to blow the lid on the Switchmen's Union and some people—and by that I mean *some people*—didn't like the idea much. And so you can imagine what I think."

"Why was he going to 'blow the lid on the Switchmen's Union?'" I asked, and the woman must have heard my stultified tone, because she looked like she was going to spit on my desk.

"Roger said something about," the woman paused, recalling, "black market goods being loaded onto freighters by certain squalid switchmen."

"What kind of black market goods?"

"He never mentioned."

She gave a harrowing account of the switchman's life, replete with dinner routine, the hour his alarm sounded each morning, his Sunday yard work. Finished and breathing hard, gray hair clinging to her forehead, she expounded some more and fell silent. Perspiration slithered on her exposed skin like she'd just enjoyed a bath of swamp water. It was disgusting to me.

"Any witnesses?" I asked.

"Just the engineer."

"What does he say?"

"He was asleep."

"So he wasn't really a witness."

"He was there," she spat.

As bluntly as I could I told her that her personal grief was not a good enough reason to suspect assassination. People get in the way of trains sometimes. "Basically I don't like or trust people who sweat profusely," I said aloud without really meaning to.

"You have the mouth of a dog," she said.

"Not every freak death is a conspiracy," I said. She tore into a plastic bag of tissues. "Stupidity is extremely unregarded as a transport to death."

"Roger wasn't stupid, if that's what you mean."

"I do, and I'm sorry, but anybody who gets his head knocked off by a slow-moving train is challenged in some special way. Wouldn't you agree?"

I could have taken her dollars and done nothing but sit around and stare at them for a week, then report to her that I'd been unable to uncover anything conclusive. Maybe I was feeling lazy; possibly, I simply did not care. From Malthus one learns that the cause of all evil and crime is overpopulation, and ever since Pinkerton it has been good private policy for someone in my line of work never to meddle with unions.

"I thought you did this kind of thing," she said, rising with tissues clasped in each hand.

"Honestly, I don't know what it is I do anymore. It's not your fault. I'm disillusioned, is all."

"It certainly isn't *mine*," she hissed. "I ought to spit right on your desk."

She sobbed out to the hallway. As the elevator descended her whelps grew distant and stopped altogether, then resumed through the open window. I watched her hustle across the street against the light, nearly getting plowed down by a dump truck.

Thinking about the easy $400 I could have acquired, I tucked in my once-white dress shirt and propped a suit coat on my shoulders. A year and a half ago I'd nailed a portrait mirror to the backside of the door. Intended as security to inspect every angle of a client, it served mainly to deflate my vanity. Not a handsome man, perhaps, rather plump and grim under the eyes, the kind of looks certain women appreciate from a distance and realize, on closer scrutiny, they are very mistaken. But I wasn't out for any woman. I'm sure they'd had enough of me, too.

Well, Harry Jome, I said to myself, stepping into the plank-floored corridor, whose walls were painted in indignant swipes of yellow and red. Let's you and me get a couple of eggs. It's about time we had some excitement.

May was humid.

The people walking the streets were dressed too warmly, and a collective grimace was growing wider by the inch, not at all helped by the pattering rain. Maybe it wasn't the weather but the fact that unhappy people were steadily coming to understand their condition. But at least in the city you don't have to be yourself 24 hours a day. Crowds of nobodies surge and swallow you in a great gulp, hustle you along to their nowhere, suck you into a maze of aimless people attempting to appear busy. If I ever decided to long for friendship I could start talking to god or get a membership in a secret society.

All the booths were taken in the diner. Eager employees and unperturbed executives were hunched together feasting on over-told stories about a certain cubicle, a shady bookkeeper, hoary bosses with a penchant for meanness. Beside me at the counter was a midget in a mustard yellow cardigan with a guitar case leaning on his leg, so that whenever he shifted, which was perpetually, he had to keep a hand on the case to straighten it.

The waitress was a mild teenager with braces and rubber bands in her short black hair, long unpainted fingernails and a demeanor so shy it would have made a pimp blush. She got my whole order wrong: the eggs were sunny-side up, the meat was ham. To her credit it was a highly unorthodox order. The coffee, at least, wasn't ginseng tea.

Next to me the midget had his head in a newspaper and I found myself contorting to read the headlines as I ate. Suddenly he shot me an eye and crumpled the paper a bit as he pivoted away. There was nothing so attractive in the headlines anyway: death, mutilation, disease, an escalating crime rate, the subtle menace of germs and defeat, rape, pillage, genocide. It was too dirty to look at.

"I come here every day," the midget said to me, folding the paper twice, "and I sit in the same place and I don't trouble anybody."

I chewed my ham, watching him shake his head. He slicked back his greasy black hair with two large-knuckled hands. Pushed the sleeves of his brown plaid jacket up past his elbows.

"I don't trouble anybody, you know?"

"Yeah, I know," I said.

"Sorry," he said. "I'm just in the mood for talking. You want to talk?"

"Talk about what?"

"You know what's funny?" he said, and answered his question: "Nothing. I can't think of a single thing that's funny." He straightened the guitar case. "Isn't that funny or sort of?"

Depressive inclinations arose as I shoveled sopping egg onto unbuttered toast. At the end of the week I would be losing my office and shortly thereafter my apartment on a sunny avenue in the 4800 block. Letters had arrived from the respective invisible landlords, warning nongrammatically that I was three months behind. If I did not pay by May 15 I would be dragged into a courtroom and divested of my car and whatever else was reputed to have some value.

I was planning to leave town as soon as I could pay for gas. Now I wished I'd accepted the railroad widow's money and fled, which wasn't too chivalrous, but poverty isn't chivalrous either. I scraped the plate clean and dusted off the driblets of food on the formica countertop.

"You know that," the midget said. "A guy like you. You work around here?"

"Upstairs in the building across the street."

"Up - stairs," he said, as two words. "I'd like to work upstairs some day. I'm a musician. I mean, I play this guitar. I'm going upstate in a week. You ever been upstate? Upstate is hell."

"Not even once."

"It's hell."

He hopped off the stool.

"I mean," he went on. "That's only the funniest thing anymore. People are different everywhere, though. Some people think I'm funny just sitting here. I don't know. I guess I am. But everybody's funny some ways. That's another thing that's funny."

"I'll nod to that," I said.

"Well, see you later if you come by again. I'm here every day, so if you're around I'll be around. Name's Leo." He grabbed his guitar case. Looked at me like he was going to tell me something else that was funny, zigzagged out of the diner.

Another cup of coffee and a slice of cherry pie. I watched the waitress open a rotating glass case, cut the pie, balance it on a plate, rush it over, slam it down, hurry back, close the glass case, wipe her hands on a dishtowel, start the process anew for some other tired louse.

Before I had a second to lift the fork someone sidled in between the stools, touching my forearm with a bony elbow. In a churlish, clear voice, a woman asked the harried waitress where she could find Henry Jome. I was so taken aback at overhearing my name that I almost fainted.

Brilliant red hair was the first thing I noticed. The questioner was a slightly attractive, narrow-faced woman of around 35 or 40. Big dark sunglasses covered what were purportedly her eyes. In profile she had slightly masculine features that lend themselves gracefully to women of a particular attitude, and she certainly had that attitude. She was in black slacks and a matching turtleneck; the pinkish tint of her skin indicated that she hadn't been in the sun for a few decades. By her subtle perfume, plush leather tote and air of astute arrogance, she was either wealthy or very wealthy. "Do you know where the office of a Mr. Jome would be? I believe it's Henry Jome?" she said.

"Who?" the waitress said over the head of a customer at the end of the counter.

"Harry Jome," I corrected.

"I'm sure it's Henry Jome," the redhead repeated. "He apparently has an office nearby."

"Excuse me," I said.

The redhead squinted at me from the corner of her frames and said, pouting her lips, "I was speaking to her if you don't mind much."

"Yes, and I'm talking to you if it's not an inconvenience."

"Well, I wish you wouldn't."

"You're asking about Harry Jome?" I said.

"I don't know that person," the waitress said.

"Except I wasn't asking you."

"I'm doing you a favor, lady."

"Well, stop it."

Once again she tried to flag the waitress' attention, but the girl was too busy arguing with the cook to notice. The waitress screamed at the beefy man in white; she pulled the apron off and hurled it onto the grill. The stench of charred cotton brought scowls among the patrons. The former waitress took advantage of the furor in the kitchen to calmly open the register and clean out the contents.

It was my first smile in 15 days.

"You see what you did?" I said to the redhead.

"I thought maybe you'd like a job." She was backing away.

"Everybody knows Harry Jome," I said. "Try the Santos Building. Take the elevator to the 3rd floor and if you survive that it's the third door on the left. If he isn't in just wait a minute."

"You his agent or something?" she asked.

"Harry is the kind of guy who doesn't even need an agent," I said.

She was out the door. Behind me two paunchy men in matching suits and porkpie hats were close behind her, pointing and hushing each other. One of them turned and winked.

The chef cursed madly while his staff wrought chaos trying to put out the small fire with glasses of water. Meanwhile, the diners filed out in search of an eatery that wasn't aflame. My coffee was drained but for a splatter of half-and-half at the bottom of the cup. I felt lonely.

I **took the elevator** to the third floor, bracing myself against the claustrophobic walls. The burnt, grimy taste of coffee swam in my mouth. I was getting a little sleepy.

The building that confined my office to its cement purgatory was one of the last authentically nasty establishments in that section of the city, a historical landmark of depravity and Prohibition-era vice. Reputedly it was due to be torn down any day now and I didn't blame whoever was doing the tearing. The Santos Building had once been renowned as a haven for desperate call girls, and the basement was said to have been a hub for all kinds of debaucheries.

The hallways of each floor had been gutted of any personality: a chair leaned in a corner, the windows covered with cardboard, pipes gurgling under your feet and in the walls. All in all, it was so seedy you had to plant your shoes when you stumbled in.

Adjacent to my stenciled, fogged-glass door was a vacant room I'd never been curious enough about. Sometimes a light was on inside, and I could distinctly hear a man singing low in a foreign language, but otherwise, I'd never seen anyone milling around the halls. The landlord himself was just a telephone number that led constantly to a phone being hung up.

My office was unlocked. I hadn't bothered to replace the knob I'd yanked off in the throes of my second marriage. Not much to steal, anyway, unless there's high demand for peeling wallpaper or bent paper-clips. The carpet that covered half the center of the floor was deeply green, paint flecked.

The redhead was already there, seated with her back to me in a chair that, 45 minutes ago, had been behind my desk. I made some noise coming into the room but she didn't seem to notice. You can figure out a lot about a person by how impervious they are to your presence.

I sauntered cooly over and sat on the edge of the desk, made a production of crossing my ankles, started sucking on a toothpick. She was prim to the point of being blatantly indifferent, hands clenched in her lap as though she were engaged in pondering the squiggles on a Pollock. Up close, her face was too wide and too hard, cheekbones prominent— the face of a film star who doesn't get too many parts. Her glasses were off now and her eyes were green, wide-set and unyielding; the rest of her attempted to prove them right.

"Hello. Remember me?" I asked.

"Do you have a cigarette?" She had a habit of speaking with her mouth compressed, as though she were training to be a ventriloquist.

"At the diner?" I said. "Remember? About three minutes ago?"

"Because I left my pack at home. And it would be nice if you had one so I don't have to go crazy."

"Sitting at the counter and—"

"Do you or don't you have a cigarette?"

"I quit a month ago."

"How'd you do that?"

"Carrots."

"They're hard to keep lit. But that's admirable of you," she said, going through the purse between her heels.

"It doesn't feel too admirable."

"Admirable things usually don't."

Very casually she extracted a plain white envelope being used as a bookmarker in a pamphlet-thin novel. On the front my name had been written in tiny cursive.

"Won't you lose your place?" I asked.

"I already read it. You know Dominic Early?" she asked.

"Maybe, but for some reason I don't really think you care what I have to say."

"Crime writer. He has a lackluster grip on the way people actually behave. Entertaining, though."

"Let's start a book club later. What's this about?"

She batted her finger on the envelope and said: "This concerns my brother Ben and needless to say it's confidential, if that means anything to you."

"Information is overvalued," I said. "Some jerk once defined hell as an infinite stream of details and possibilities. If that means anything to you."

"It doesn't."

She flung the envelope on my lap. It slipped onto the floor and I bent and grabbed it.

"There's a check inside for eight thousand dollars," she said.

"I don't like surprises anyway."

"Do you like personal checks?"

At that point I would have accepted muskrat hides. I unsealed the envelope with a greedy finger and greeted the digits inside.

"Susan K. Longtree," I read.

Susan K. Longtree looked at me over the tip of her pert nose.

"Just don't call me Susan," she said. "Nor think of me using that name."

"What's the K stand for?"

"It's silent."

I loosened the knot on my tie, peering like a creep at her pomaded red hair and everything else, trying so hard not to look desperate that the effort was pure desperation.

"My brother, Ben," she started. "He killed himself two weeks ago in a motel up north." She related it in a mechanical spurt, the way you might tell the plumber that the faucet is broken. Something tugged at her lips now, not tears but the opposite of tears. "Ben was married to a woman here in the city and had a kid with her—a girl, Dot. So what I'm saying, Mr. Jome, is that Ben did not lead a miserable life. He worked as a golf instructor in that club outside of town. Family. Job."

"Sometimes both in collaboration can ruin anyone. The wife wasn't troubled by his mental state?"

"Carol and I haven't ever gotten along. For that matter, neither have Ben and I. He was always happier than I was."

"I take it you never noticed anything foul?"

"Not so much."

I let the tension stir the room until she was forced to look at me again. "What exactly, Ms. Longtree, is it you're here for?"

Sue Longtree looked at me with blank eyes.

"I'm wondering. Ben didn't leave a note," she said. "Is that strange?"

"Not really. I've tried writing in suicidal anguish. It's all romantic slop and not well phrased."

She glared at me, not altogether sure whether I was being facetious or sincere. I wasn't exactly sure myself.

"So I would like to hire your services for a few days or a

week and hopefully find out why Ben did it. Could there possibly be a note somewhere?"

"Is that all there is?" I said.

"Just like the song says."

I scribbled in an unlined reporter's notebook. The short-hand looked like a screwed-up association game, the hasty marks of a messy hieroglyphics only I could decipher.

"The eight thousand is a down payment," she said. "Essentially, I don't care how he died. If a person kills himself for no reason, a sibling is liable to get worried. Genes and whatnot. Believe me, I'm not paranoid. If Ben killed himself for a bona fide purpose, all right. As I said before: Find out why. And it's Mrs. Longtree. That's why I'm not able to research for myself. I'm going through a divorce that ought to be settled in a trench."

"I'm awfully busy right now," I said.

"No," she said. "You're not."

I poured myself a soda water I'd been saving and asked the woman if she wanted some.

"I'll take some rum," she said.

"No rum."

"What do you have?"

"I have some soda water."

I paced and drank while she talked. The story of her brother wasn't terribly riveting stuff. Sue and Ben were both born upstate, the only offspring of Daddy and Mrs. Longtree.

"What's your father's name?" I asked.

"That's it."

"What's it?"

"His name is Daddy."

"I don't think you're being serious."

"If he had any other name we never knew it."

Their father ran a once prosperous orchard five or more hours north. Soon after Sue was born, Mrs. Longtree took the kids to live in the city away from Daddy and the isolation.

"My mother loved the city and my father loves the orchard," Sue said. "So it caused some conflict. We visited the orchard sometimes. I couldn't stand the place. Ben and I spent a lot of time together up there when we were kids, sneaking around, ducking out at night."

"What about Daddy?" I asked.

"He was always holed up at the orchard. Daddy wasn't

anything more than a presence for me. After a while we stopped going to see him because he was getting weird. Nobody really missed him."

The fast crack of Sue's voice was somehow transfixing, like being punched in the face with a peppermint leaf.

"At 17," Sue went on, "I traveled awhile, thinking myself some kind of itinerant writer. I met my currently estranged husband at a lounge in Chicago. He manages and conducts a big band. They're called The Boys and the music is so bad it's demeaning for me to stoop to criticize it."

"Well, you did marry him," I said.

"Yes," she said. "Marriage definitely is an institution."

For Sue the rest was lawyers, estate debacles and a third-rate future of uncertainty in and reliance on despised money. She glossed over the personal details, and though there was some pain in her voice it was the suffering of being snapped with a rubber band at close quarters.

Meanwhile, Ben Longtree had packed off to university. Before he received his degree in biology, however, he suddenly quit and continued his career as a golfer. He won some high-paying tournaments and was interviewed a few times on the radio. At 35 he stopped competing and got himself a job at a country club outside of town. It was there that he met his wife, Carol Bergen, a tobacco heiress. That was five years ago.

"He took his wife's name," Sue said scornfully. "Bergen. I don't understand how he could be so weak."

"Maybe he loved her," I offered

Sue scoffed.

"I didn't change my name when I got married."

"Maybe you didn't love him," I offered again.

"Anyway," she said. "Carol is an abomination."

So Ben Bergen drove north into the hills around Sutter Falls to drop in for their father's 67th birthday. A day later he was found in his motel room, the radio blaring (the maid recounted), a neat hole through the roof of his mouth, out the top of his head and embedded in the crook of the plaster ceiling. Immediately the slaying was ruled self-slaughter and no one doubted the verdict, especially not Sue Longtree.

"They didn't so much as dust the door handle," she said. "It might have been quick, but these are the sorts of towns that have nothing to do except cart away suicides and bargain with housewives not to send two barrels into their husbands."

"What about Daddy? You said Ben was up there to see him."

Sue took a long look at her red-painted fingernails.

"According to the police Ben never showed up there."

"And your mother?"

"Dead. She was sleepwalking one night and tossed herself out our 12-story window. While ago."

"Another suicide," I said.

Across the room a rat poked its slick head from a fissure in the baseboard, saw me, froze, and disappeared back into the hole.

"So," I said to break the silence, squinting at my chaotic notation. "Bergen leads a fulfilling existence. Underwhelming job, wife and daughter. And so on. One night he just kills himself. It's definitely not murder, and nothing so far as you can tell is nefarious about the incident. You'd like me to look at the death for any indication that it could be the result of a destructive tendency in your family, some bad gene or what- ever." I paused, drank, let the soda water fizz under my tongue. "So, OK."

"There's one other thing," she said. "It could be nothing. But Ben signed in at the hotel under a different name. William Florence."

"That's not so crazy," I said, pacing behind her so that she had to twist to follow me.

"Why isn't that so crazy?" she asked.

I shrugged. "People rarely behave like they should when they're about to shoot themselves. It probably doesn't mean anything."

"So you'll look into this?" Sue asked.

"I guess so, until it leads nowhere or somewhere."

"I appreciate that," she said. She clasped the mouth of her purse and slipped it over her shoulder. "Everything you need is written on the envelope. Phone numbers. Addresses. I'd contact Carol first and I'd do it before noon. She has her own time zone, and it's always time for a drink there. Then Ben's boss at the club, and maybe—"

"I'll take care of it," I said.

We shook hands. Her palm was as dry as a whale bone.

I handed her one of my last business cards. A ring of cof- fee encircled the upper left hand corner.

"I like your logo," she said, nodding at the stain.

"I had it specially made."

"I can't show any emotion. People tell me that all the time. It doesn't bother me anymore."

She gave me one glance in the mirror, then was out the door before I could respond.

For a while I thought about her red hair, her arctic demeanor. In some sick way I liked her lack of concern and expensive rancor. When you begin to care is when the war marches and the beach guns start.

Gently, I folded the check in equal halves, drooling. I was thinking of nothing but the money and how it touched me just right where I needed to be touched.

I put a hat on my head and flicked the light switch. The hall was soundless and barren, some dust and plaster floating onto the carpet. The rusted grates of the elevator clanged shut, and the heap descended. I counted my check in a better light, the paper crisp and impersonal and modern. The feeling it induced, however, was positively prehistoric.

After cashing the check and stuffing the fifties and twenties in my pocket, wrapped in a little plastic bag, I went to a pawn shop that specialized in my hocked goods. The metallic guts of the shop were congested with unwanted silverware and thick dust. I purchased back the pistol that I'd brought in a week ago, when my pecuniary status had been drastic. The proprietor was a smart-ass Hungarian with a beard that would have made fungi jealous. He had one of the largest collections of harmonicas in the world, like a wandering harmonica orchestra had passed through town down on its luck. The Hungarian wished me a happy death when I was exiting his shop. "Which is all that life is for," he elaborated.

I wasn't sure exactly why buying back my weapon was so important, only that I felt bereft without it, a man deprived of a primary tool of his art.

I walked in the rain as excited as a dumb child at a horse race. My newfound cash was rolled into my right fist, my free hand caressing the gun in my pocket. Around 30th I started perusing shop windows, the way saps do when they've just received a modest sum of dollars and need to consider how it should be squandered.

At a delicatessen I bought a wheel of cheese and a yardstick of Italian salami. The rain was starting to come down forcefully as I reached 48th Street. I didn't have an umbrella. Rain always felt good on my skin. Maybe it was a prenatal thing.

My apartment complex was a series of three plain buildings designed around an uncared-for park. The grass hadn't been cut in months, the trees gnarled and perishing. No one wanders the unappealing, graffiti-stained path. As for the architecture of the buildings, it could be characterized as frigid Bauhaus in its charmlessness. My neighborhood is somewhere in limbo, inhabited by a people of no extreme inclinations or ambitions, drifted along by a son of a bitch of a god whose idea of fun is leaving us to writhe and argue and die. Just like anybody else anywhere else.

The mail slot for 201 housed three Chinese take-out menus and a letter that had been there for three years, from a girl I didn't want to remember and a time I didn't want to forget. She was a short, dour girl who'd left me in a phone booth waiting for her for three hours. Later I found out that she'd gone to San Francisco and married a yacht and the guy who owned it. She could have been the only lady I cared anything for.

Inside my apartment I stored the cheese, the salami and the money in the icebox. It was a little after four.

A row of bookshelves was arranged chronologically on one wall in the living room; mostly the titles were related to late medieval philosophy, Aquinas' works, the collected essays on magic by Bruno, Eckhardt's surreal dreams about creepy angels who visited him during the night.

The furniture in the room was sparse, an armchair with a leather footstool, a sofa under the bay window, glass-topped coffeetable scattered with shabby magazines. Likewise, the kitchen's utility was based solely around an oblong table and one oak chair. As for the bedroom, it was a place where I slept. It held a big bed and was so practical I could have been denounced as a communist.

I checked on the money in the icebox, where it was chilled and hardening, the way money should be. I drew a bath and soaked awhile, pondering Sue's hair and other attributes. Afterwards I ran a razor over my face and sprinkled on some minty lotion. I laid on the crumpled sheets of the bed. A poplar brushed the window sympathetically. Poplars do that.

The unlikely suicide of Sue Longtree's brother was still a

shapeless, random event that had no meaning. I liked Sue Longtree a bit, but probably the more I enjoyed her ruthlessness the less I would enjoy her ruthlessness.

The pillow was terribly inviting and dreams were fitful; in them I died at least twice. I awoke, having slept all of 25 minutes.

Later that evening I had dinner in solitude, joined by the sputtering static of a black and white television set rambling on with an idiotic advertisement. I got one channel. Better than silence.

As I polished off a cheese and salami sandwich I flipped the pages of my notebook, decoding the unintelligible script. Very little actual information to go on, but it was enough for the moment.

The heading of the first page was printed: *Sue Longtree, client* and underneath that:

Ben Bergen (used the name "William Florence"), suicide, no note, motel in Sutter Falls

Carol Bergen, wife of BB, call on immediately

Dot Bergen, daughter

Shady Palm Country Club, BB employed, interview manager (Montero)

Contact Pol. Dept. in Sutter Falls

Mrs. Longtree, killed self in sleep (the immortality of dreams?)

Daddy Longtree, father of Sue and Ben, hermit, BB visited shortly before.

Below that, in the margin of the page, I had misspelled the word *Orchard* and even when I had it right, the word looked off.

E arly on Wednesday morning I showered and threw on a white shirt, the brown suit and black wingtips. I polished the shoes while they were on my feet, spending a good five minutes on each one. I'd owned them since a senior dance in high school, and the area just in back of the toes was as creased as a cutting board. Some Beethoven quartet was winding down on the record player.

In the bathroom mirror my reflection had drastically improved over the past day or so. My hair had changed over to gray when I was 22, a semester into medieval studies, and had not recuperated since. Sometimes it lent a grave dignity to my poor, sullen face. Frankly, I was exhilarated to be working again, and the case fascinated me because it made no overtures to being eventful. I smiled at myself, and the smile was nearly authentic.

I scrubbed the dishes in the sink while my toast burned. Sang off-key at the radio, had a couple bites of cereal. I brought the toast with me into the taxi, wrapped in a napkin. The bald, unhealthy-looking driver scowled at me in the rearview, muttering at the steering wheel in a volley of whispered complaints that I believed were directed at me.

Whole parts of the city were nothing but trash. Clenched in the early rush of vehicles, I looked at the streets heaped with unappealing black bags. People were hurling refuse indiscriminately onto the sidewalk now. Wrappers, beer cans, egg cartons, all manner of comestibles, soaked from the rain and strewn in parking lots and in lawns. Rotting meat was prevalent, its sunset-pink juices draining into the gutter. Some folks had attempted to drive their trash to the public landfill outside of town but were turned back: the big stinking crater in the ground was filled to capacity. Further digging had commenced. They would never be done digging. Maybe that's the end to all outwardly impressive cultures.

The driver and I made a few snide quips at the extravagant neighborhood. He beat a fast left onto 3rd to outpace a light.

Carol Bergen's house was near the middle of the block on the wide, cedar-lined boulevard, number 113, with a cast-iron woodpecker for a mailbox. Two sculpted bushes guarded the driveway.

I handed the driver fare plus a ten.

"You ain't got to be cocky about it," he said.

Compared to the ultra-modern monstrosities that formed the rest of the block, the Bergen residence was almost Victorian. Lattice-work ran the length of the flaking brown-stone facade, shoots of vine grappling at the white criss-crossed planks. The walkway was red brick, the air infused with the dense sweetness of wet grass. A shiny car half poked out of the garage, and golf clubs were scattered in the yards.

I rang the bell and a dull chime flirted out of tune with a standard hymn. A white, monotonous sky held an airplane. Before I could press the bell a second time a woman had the door ajar, swaying in a liquored, stumbling dance. A recently lit cigarette dangled out of her thin lips, and when she grinned it hit the floor. I stamped it out for her.

"Come on in," she said, the woman's eyes puffy, drowsy. "It's raining all over you."

"Mrs. Bergen?" I removed my hat and paused on the mat.

"Come on in," she repeated lightheartedly. "Whoever you are you can't be any worse."

"I might be a little worse. The light isn't so good."

"You live around here?" she inquired, emphasizing each word.

I said that I could barely afford to knock on doors in this neighborhood.

"Then you can't be any worse," she said. "Something happens to people around here. They get dull and find ways to scare one another. I'm from Minneapolis originally."

"Decent town," I said.

"Is it really?" she asked gravely. "I don't remember much about it. I lived with an evil aunt who collected these hideous monkey figurines she claimed were from Egypt. Why do you ask?"

"I didn't ask."

"Why didn't you?"

Carol Bergen was a short, scrawny woman in a white linen shirt that fit her like a drape. Somewhere embroiled in her forties, unmistakably shaken, a person who is born twitchy.

The lines in her sallow face were an ideal slope for tears. Her breath was a high percentage and to whichever label it belonged it was working.

"I'm Harry Jome," I said.

She pronounced my name familiarly, as though we'd gone to middle school together.

"You sister-in-law contacted me to see what I could make of your husband's suicide."

Mrs. Bergen winced at the mention of her husband, muttering only, "Oh," and a beat later, "Why?"

"I'm not awfully sure. But sometimes it pays to not be awfully sure. Mrs. Longtree essentially wants to know the reason for his demise, whether it's in the blood or what it is." I shrugged. "So, now you know as much as I do."

Downcast and confused, she offered to take my coat and hat, and when I declined, she insisted on helping me out of my coat and hat and clutched my coat and hat in her bony arms. She tottered into the walls as she led me through a foyer. Blank, faded spots were on the walls, where photographs or watercolors had once been.

The kitchen at the end of the hallway was a cluttered mess of grimy dishes, blackened pots, cabinets disarrayed. Mrs. Bergen plunked my coat and hat on one of the chairs and poured two glasses of clear liquid from an unmarked bottle. Turned, I could see that the seat of her tan pants was patterned in coffee grounds. With her back to me she looked healthy and almost sexy. When she turned and seemed to guess my thoughts I found myself mourning the last eight or so years of her life with her. Every movement she made was misery disguised as movement.

Her body swayed clownishly as she tried to find the chair that I was positioning under her. She grimaced at me as though she had just swallowed half a decanter of melted plastic. Taped to the refrigerator was a finished crossword puzzle.

"Nice work," I said, pointing at it.

She slid into the chair inch by inch. I took the chair opposite. Mrs. Bergen pushed one of the glasses over to my side, cutting a swath through anthills of cigarette ash.

"Ben and I did that the night before, I guess, and by the way what're you doing here?"

"I'm here about Mr. Bergen—Ben."

"Ben's not here."

"Ms. Longtree sent me over."

I noticed that Mrs. Bergen's exuberant brown hair was a wig. It slipped forward over an eyebrow, revealing close-cropped gray bangs.

"Bitch," Mrs. Bergen mouthed. "You want to know something?"

She looked at the ceiling, at a loss for what she was going to say.

"How did Ben act toward the end?" I asked.

Her head snapped back down. "I don't like these questions."

"They're the only ones I brought."

"Let me apologize," she said. "There something wrong with your glass? Prefer whiskey or vodka or something?"

"I don't drink."

"What, were you raised by Quakers?" she snarled as though I had just insulted her first cousin.

"No," I said. "Alcoholics."

She laughed and hissed at the same time, lighting another cigarette and sticking it instantly into an ashtray, wrong end first. "Sometimes I think I'm better than anybody in the world." She closed her eyes for a while. Downed her drink fast. Her eyes flicked back open and she leaned across the table. "Let me tell you something, Harry Jome, or whoever I'm talking to," she whispered.

I put my head closer. Carol rose halfway out of her seat, knocking over her empty glass, and pulled my head roughly toward her waiting mouth. Close up, the mix of booze and fruity shampoo was a sickening combination. The kiss was malicious. Pulling sloppily away from me, she plunked back into place, crying suddenly and softly.

"Why'd you do that?" she asked. "I mean, I'm sorry, I didn't mean to do that."

"You thought I was somebody else," I said.

"I guess you're right," she said.

"I'm just here about Ben."

"Excuse me while I go away for a moment to compose myself."

She oscillated into the next room. My stopping by was worthless and sorrowful. An untoward kindness came over me and I put her glass in the sink, then lifted my hat and coat on. Passing by the living room I saw that she had fallen asleep on the orange corduroy sofa, her restless body twitching in a nightmare that would be right where she'd left it. One of her sad eyes opened and she murmured, "I'm better than everyone else in the world, except for—" and didn't finish plagiarizing herself.

High above the couch there was a drawing of an orchard that I barely glanced at and would have forgotten had it not been so strikingly out of place in a room with no other pictures. The style was expressionistic and influenced by twilight, similar to a Goya print or a print by a friend of Goya's.

So far the only thing I knew about Ben Bergen was that he had been alive and now he wasn't.

I shut the front door silently behind me just as Carol Bergen belched in her sleep.

Considering Mrs. Bergen's overall condition, it suddenly hit me that Sue Longtree's inquiry was absurd. What was she expecting me to find out? Why? Did it make any difference if you knew as definitive that you were crazy and that you'd been crazy from the start? Plus, Sue didn't care a lot about the fate of her brother, only how it impinged on her. Still, eight grand was a tidy sum I couldn't pass up, even if I wasn't too sure what I was passing up and what I was holding onto.

Strong winds were racing in from the east and I had to wrestle all the way to the Santos Building, sweating when I reached the downstairs lobby. As usual, nobody was around. The stairwell was gray and dank, haunted by a deathly stale scent. A puddle had formed on the second-floor landing and I hopped over the little pool.

I rummaged through my drawers for nothing in particular. I was anxious, confined; the euphoria of the morning had been beaten to death by Carol Bergen's pathos. I kind of felt bad for her because I knew what it was like to wage a fruitless struggle against the bottle. And maybe a little affectionate, too. Mrs. Bergen was an apt cliche, and cliches are dangerous, because they're generally so appropriate.

In the drawers I picked out a bullet that had been mailed to me by an incapable man in the heat of his divorce; a counterfeit $100 bill; antacid tablets; a candy bar that had liquefied and solidified so frequently that the silver wrapping was probably more edible; $1.27 in loose change; the degree I'd earned at a stuffy haven of higher learning; one shelled cashew; and nine street maps of the city. A snooping biographer would have all the details he would ever need to write the life of Harry Jome, and then he'd quit and tell his publisher it didn't amount to much—an article if he was lucky, and could he have a few spare bucks for the work, to keep things genuine, because anybody who would write about me would necessarily be the kind of person who was often broke. I dusted out the lint, replaced the junk, and was squeezing myself into a mild depression when the phone rang.

"Jome," I said into the receiver.

"You sound uncertain about that," Sue Longtree said.

"Just a little low. Your sister-in-law is a six-a.m. drunk. There's not much I can do with her. Even tried to seduce me, I think. She's got a lot of problems."

"I wonder if she's still my sister-in-law," Sue said musingly. "With Ben dead and everything."

"Would you like me to find that out too?"

"Saying something dumb isn't the same as wit."

"Wit is too profound for me. I usually just bounce my head against the wall for kicks."

Sue cleared her throat.

"You know," I said. "You haven't really told me why you suspect this preposterous theory about your family."

"Both my grandparents were suicides. At the same time."

"Double suicides are as rare as twins."

"Just as hard to feed, too."

"Ms. Longtree, I think maybe—"

"You're going a little short on my prefix, Mr. Jome. Did I tell you I'm married?"

"I must not have been listening. There was a lot to look at and I might have ignored that knowledge."

I held the phone in the crook of my shoulder and took it for a walk to the window. Another dreary, pitiable day that had no ambition, the kind of sky that made you want to build a better one.

"I haven't traced my genealogy far, but what I know is that there is cause to worry."

"What you need is someone to let you talk and cry and stuff."

She laughed and it was horrendous. "Everybody has a shrink nowadays," she said. "You give him a problem and he gives you some cute little yellow pills to help remember your childhood differently."

I thought of her hair draped lugubriously over the phone. Red hair always bothered me, and by that I mean it has never bothered me.

"Besides," she said. "What would you do if you were me? It's possible that I'm a threat to myself or other people. If you can get evidence I'll check myself into the nearest blue ward a second later."

"This isn't going anywhere."

"A happy person does not kill himself is all I am saying, and from what I know my family has a tendency toward killing themselves."

A taut silence ensnared itself on the line.

"Well," I said. "OK then."

"Goodbye, Mr. Jome."

Sue Longtree was pretty, dedicated, endearingly eccentric. She reminded me of someone I'd like a lot. She was nuts, but she wore it well, and she was also smart, but smart is an acquired trait, and occasionally a tad dangerous. She was something else. I couldn't say what.

Down below in the rain-puttering street a person shouted as loud as he could, as though the shrill message was intended solely for my edification.

Beside the entry in my notebook marked *Carol Bergen* I wrote *drunk, uncooperative, enticing*. Underneath Sue Longtree I jotted *nuts* and couldn't conjure anything more definitive about her. It was quite an extant list that could have easily meant nothing at all.

I propped the window and rested my elbows on the sill. In the jumbled fog of the distant hills a despondent spot of blue sky was intruding; within seconds it was not there and the gray was everywhere in view. Short, angular skyscrapers glinted insipidly. Further off to the east the bridge over the river was spindly and delicate, far away and no more than a future—or past perfect—tense.

Straight down below on the street a dog scurried by trying to catch the raindrops in its gaping mouth.

I dialed information and the operator connected me to the Sutter Falls Police, which was probably two guys in straw hats arguing over who's going to sit shotgun in front of the desk fan. A breathy woman breathed that no one was available to talk. I gave her my office number and she muttered that someone would return my call later that afternoon or tomorrow. If she said goodbye I didn't hear it.

I put the recently un-hocked pistol in the drawer, wondering if I should keep it with me but resolving that I probably wouldn't need it for quite a while.

I acted like I was locking my office and headed for the stairs when I noticed the stationary shadow around a bend in the hallway, with grimy loafers. I slammed the stairwell door and the shadow recessed, dragging a man out of the darkness. He was at least 45, obese and panting, taller than me by a couple of inches. The only hair on his head beneath a loud porkpie hat was coming out of his nostrils. A flamboyant green silk shirt was unbuttoned to the collarbone beneath a plaid suit.

He saw me fast but not as fast as he would have liked.

"You're lost," I said.

"I'm lost," he stammered, his hands supplicating. "I think I am, yeah."

I took a step toward him. He replicated my movement backward.

"What're you looking for?" I asked.

"A tobacconist."

"Not here you're not."

"You mean there isn't a tobacconist's here?"

"Far as I know they don't even exist anymore."

"I guess I must be in the wrong building. What's the address here?" he asked.

"The wrong one," I said.

"Is it 227?"

"You look like you're not looking for a tobacconist's," I said.

"Is this 227?"

We stared at one another until integrity was inescapable.

"Go right ahead," I said, cocking my head at my office. "It's unlocked. It's never locked. Not sure what you expect to find."

"What is?" he asked, mock confusion staining his red jowls. "What is unlocked? You joking or just kidding?"

"The office, you worm."

Anger and sweat dripped from his big chin.

"Just leave your card on the desk in case something's missing," I said.

He was so flabbergasted he was amused. Pressing the elevator button, he said, "You have some dire problems, friend, and I'm not sure that they can be corrected."

"You muddled or something? You're blushing like a virgin. You want to ransack my office, so ransack my office. Don't let's make theater out of it. I'm just curious to see what you're looking for."

Too bothered to wait for the elevator, the guy made for the stairs. While he descended I stood at the top, peering down at his hand clutching the railing of the cross-hatched stairwell.

Between landings he said, "Fuck you."

"Sue doesn't trust me? She had to hire another dick?"

"You always fucking treat strangers like this?" he yelled back up.

"Only ones who like to hide in the shadows where they don't belong."

"Look, I fucking been around tougher than you, so," he shouted up. His voice had lost its timbre and was now a bland echo. "Why don't you get a new fucking shirt?" he said.

"I'd borrow yours but I think the Navy is using it to do maneuvers," I called. By then it was like I was talking to myself.

"Fuck you," he screamed.

"Come back and see me sometime. You impress me with your vocabulary."

"Fuck you again," he said, almost inaudibly. The man was making a Broadway hit out of two syllables. "And I mean it this—" he said, the rest of his tiny soliloquy cut short by his exit.

Thursday morning was a long, unvaried stream of curt phone calls and abrupt answers that didn't lead anywhere. Before I spoke to anyone else, it was imperative that I speak to Bergen's widow. Sometime after nine I dialed Mrs. Bergen—it was a lovely number and I had it memorized. A slab of meat was sizzling in the background, bubbling close to the phone.

"Yeah?" Mrs. Bergen hollered, then, cupping the receiver: "Dot, you stop it, goddamnit. What do you think you're doing that for?" and back in my ear. "Hello?" A kid started crying.

She sounded relatively sober. I hung up and rushed over.

Daylight was a premature baby as it dangled in the trash-filled crevasses of the city and did nothing but wax gray and forbidding. Frightened hobos rooted around in garbage bags left on porches, unsuccessfully warded off by stingy proprietors and the rare intrepid patrolman. The cab I was in stopped at a light change and I was hypnotized by the freak show outside that replayed wherever your eye wandered. Every city is alike, and the people, too. Only thing that varies in an urban ditch like this is the amount of traffic on a weekday. I loved hating the place, and I hated myself, too, for carrying it around with me.

The Bergen residence was in the same condition as I'd left it the day before, golf clubs glinting in the short grass, a Mercedes stuffed in the garage. Now the pink bicycle was orphaned on the walkway. I knocked instead of pressing the buzzer.

Carol Bergen pulled the door back and let out a draft of steamy air from inside. She was in tan slacks and her brown wig was properly on. Minus a glass of liquor in her hand she looked naked, wholly depressed at having nothing for her hands to do. Her crazed eyes were apparently not the product of booze at the moment, but something much older and deeper.

"It's possible," she said lackadaisically, "but I'm not convinced we've met." She eyed me like I was a boulder that had just rolled onto her doorstep.

I introduced myself for the second time in so many days.

"Am I interrupting?" I asked.

"I was thinking. So, yes."

"Feeling any better?"

"Why shouldn't I be feeling any better?"

"Your sister-in-law hired me to look at Mr. Bergen's suicide. I mentioned this to you, but I'm not sure you were here when I stopped by yesterday."

The little girl, Dot, was at the door now and stood looking at me with big, wondrous brown eyes. In her left hand she had a discolored blanket, and in her right she was holding a highball glass poured to the rim with milk.

"Go play somewhere," Carol said.

Dot watched me for another ten seconds and slinked off, leaving her blanket in the alcove.

"She's a good person," Carol said of her daughter. "Quiet, though. It's scary sometimes."

"Would she have anything to say about Ben?"

"Sshh," she said harshly, turning to glance down the hallway. "My daughter is minding her business and she doesn't want to hear about her father."

Carol Bergen shut the door quietly and crouched on the uppermost of the front steps, protected from the rain by an overhanging, shingle roof. Huddled, arms crossed, she seemed more petite when not drinking, 5'2" or 5'3", less than 100 pounds. I stood where I was on the porch, wondering if she would try to suck my lips away again, desiring somewhat that she would.

The breeze messed up in her hair. "Why is Sue prying?" she asked.

"This seems important to her."

"Ben hated her. Ben didn't hate anybody. But he hated her. Of course, you must have noticed that she isn't normal."

"In what way?"

"In every way."

Nearby a swing set creaked on busted hinges. Obnoxious voices of bird and human mounted in unintelligible tandem, and the rain was hitting the tips of my shoes.

I said, "Whatever Ms. Longtree is, she's curious about

Ben's death and that's all I'm doing here."

"Is it?" Carol asked sardonically. "Is that what she asked you to find out?"

"So why do you think Ben smashed himself all up?"

"You talk like your ideas were put through a meat grinder," she said, lighting a cigarette. The wind blew the smoke into my nostrils. "He was happy," she said in a low voice.

"How happy was he?"

"Is there a measurement of happiness?"

"In this example, yes."

"And what's this an example of?"

"Whatever you tell me it is, I suppose."

She inhaled and peered at the lit tip of her cigarette for a few seconds.

"He was fine."

"That's the extent of it?"

A curl of her wig hooked into a doleful eye and she swiped it away with the pinkie of the hand waving the cigarette. She puckered her lips in an attempt to refrain from saying anything important or insulting, and then resumed. "That's the extent of him," she said.

"Depressed? Agitated?"

"Ben worked four days a week at the club," she said, exhaling a laborious plume of smoke. "We had arguments over money, the color of the carpet, the worthlessness of the maid. Never when Dot was in the house, though. On Saturdays the three of us went shopping for groceries—you know, apples, tomato sauce, salted butter. That sort of thing. Our sex life was ordinary, since I suspect that's one of your forthcoming questions. Ben voted in major elections. He loved swimming at the Y and talked about the area near his father's place. Vacation twice a year, usually to my family's cottage in North Carolina. Sometimes to Key West. In 15 years of marriage we experienced approximately 10 months of misery from each other. And that's adding up every second. Not so bad, huh?"

"Sounds like you're reciting from a movie treatment."

"I thought that's what you wanted."

"I do. I wasn't complaining. Ever meet his father? Daddy?"

"Once about eight or nine years ago. I didn't like him. He was creepy. The whole place is creepy. There was something weird between him and Ben but I don't know what it was." She shook her head and straightened the wig.

"Something to do with Sue, you think?"

"I wouldn't know."

"What did Ben think of him?"

"He hardly mentioned him unless he was drinking, and that was rare. When he drank he told stories about the orchard and his sister and all that."

"How about the orchard?"

"Nothing about. Ben was happy up there, and when he went to visit Daddy for the last time—" She broke off and plucked nonexistent dirt from the knee of her pants, then continued. "From what I can tell he liked it up there, but his relationship to Daddy I couldn't tell you much about. Like I said, something between them was off."

Carol Bergen extinguished her cigarette on the sole of her black flat and tucked the butt in her pants pocket.

"You're kind of callous, aren't you?" she said.

"This isn't too complicated, Mrs. Bergen," I said.

"It was nice of you to stop in," she said, rising to her feet, using one arm for balance. "I have to go check on Dot, make sure she hasn't started taking after me."

"Maybe I can help you," I said, and it sounded dumber than I imagined it could.

"With what?"

"With whatever you need."

"You're cute," she said. "You're so cute you make me wheeze. Go bother somebody else now."

"Perhaps you wouldn't mind telling me something truthful about your late husband," I said.

She had her hand on the knob. "He's not late. He's dead. Is that truthful enough?"

"It might be," I said.

"It has to be," she said.

She burned the end of a fresh cigarette and took a short, nervous puff.

"It's not that I care overly much," I said. "Don't worry about me getting too close to anything."

"You couldn't get close to a balloon. And I don't care either. I have to go inside now."

The kid was standing there as she swung the door open and closed it. Another squandered nice afternoon. I was lethargic and didn't know where to go with this business. No one could tell me anything important, except for the fact that everyone I was dealing with was crazy or learning how to be.

From within the house I could hear Carol yelling at Dot, and the kid not replying. Must have been hard cohabitating with a quiet child. Then I heard bottles clinking together. After that the house was domestic and quiet from the outside.

A fancy silver car idled by as I was stepping away from the house. The driver's hand waved out the open window at me, mistaking me for a friend or at the very least somebody who would wave back at him.

I waved back.

I went to the office for a while and thought and the thinking didn't amount to much save to exhaust me. I sprawled on the sofa in the dark. Sounds came from the building, from below me, and I tried picking them apart and locating their origin. One sounded like someone trying to push a statue out of his way, and another—a grating echo— was the noise of a thousand hurrying ants amplified. I was shortly sleeping a sleep that wasn't really sleep, but more like a shutting down of awareness, and each time I snapped awake I was hyper and ready.

Dreams were wayward and sick. Men positioned on rooftops carried small toy guns. Garbage bags hurtled from tall windows, the inhabitants of the city unseen. And the balding fat man who'd tried to creep into my office appeared at every intersection brandishing a shotgun.

"Can you spare a mink?" he asked confidentially. "Or can't you."

"What do you want a mink for?" I asked him.

"Or can't you," he repeated nastily.

Then the nightmare turned fine: I was horizontal on a bed in Sue Longtree's boudoir, engaged in a euphemism that is typically followed by childrearing. Sue kept morphing into all the women I had known over the years. Frankly, it was distasteful, but succubi rarely behave like ladies. Just before culmination I was alone, the shouts of the women ringing in my ears. I was sprawled on a dirt highway and the orchard was on the horizon. The place was in black and white, char- coal and ink, exactly as it was in the drawing at the Bergen place. I rarely recalled my dreams, but this one was especially memorable. I was stirred awake at dawn by a mis-timed alarm clock in the next office that wouldn't shut off. I banged the walls with my fists and the noise finally subsided and someone on the other side of the wall groaned and let out an irritated, "OK. *Jesus.*"

Grappling with consciousness I had a great desire to sock

my id in the jaw. Hot air stirred in the office. There was a presence in the close room that I attributed to the garbled dreams that hadn't felt like my own. I'd been in and out of sleep for four hours.

"Who is it?" I said to the emptiness.

I was still in my coat and the rain from the folds had seeped into the sofa. Without many prospects I grabbed the Dominic Early novel from my desk and staggered out into the hallway. I listened for the others I knew must have been in the building—where had that alarm clock come from?—but the only sound was of my heightened listening.

I took a cab to my apartment and leaned my head into the icebox to cool off, peeling back a bountiful bunch of frigid $20 bills.

I called Sue Longtree and told her to meet me at the bar around the corner, Hank's, in about a half hour.

"Why?" she asked. "You have something?"

"I don't like eating breakfast alone," I said. "And you need to tell me some more about this."

"I've told you everything I can."

"Then make up some stories and tell me those."

I stripped in the bathroom, showered, lathering myself with a bar of soap I'd been saving for the occasion. The hot water was good and I was starting to lean into wakefulness. I had two black suits in my wardrobe, one with a button missing and one that was too narrow at the shoulders. I chose the button missing variation. A new suit was the epitome of what I needed right then, and I decided to pay a visit to Cramm, a cheap tailor who wasn't too bad with thread.

I clicked a record onto the player in the corner, Bartok I think it was. Violins screaming in lonely synchrony, but it discomfited me and I took the Early book with me when I left. I had a few minutes to spare.

As I came down the stairs someone scurried out the door, but I didn't think much of it. I put $900 in the landlord's slot. It was raining like the sky had gone mad, and maybe it had, and I stuck close to the awnings of buildings as I went.

Hank's was a bare 24-hour restaurant and bar that was well-known for serving homemade fruitcake in all seasons and for hosting underground poker marathons. Three gamblers, not counting the guy face-down, were playing hands of Texas Hold-Em, and they looked to have not rested in five or six days, and in Hank's it was probable that they had not.

I ordered sausage links and toast from Hank, a droopy-eyed Austrian who could play anything on the accordion except a right note. He was in a red shirt and tan trousers covered in variegated hues of paint. He took my order and didn't say anything.

Early's book was called *An Incidental Murder*, and it was a supremely silly tale about a private detective who tries to shoot himself, misses his head by an inch, and accidentally kills the guy in the next apartment. As far as plots went it was muddled and fragmentary, and by Chapter 12 I was glad to pick up my head and see Sue hurry by the window, close her umbrella as she came into the restaurant, and glance around for me.

All of the gamblers but the unconscious guy perked up quickly at her entrance, eyes prowling her curves, and immediately deflated when Sue sat across from me. Her hair was tied back with a ribbon, nails freshly painted red, and her smile was one I could have sucked out of a straw.

"You like that nonsense?" she asked of the dog-eared novel in front of me.

"It's daft," I said. "Pointless. Drab."

"You should be a critic."

"Who says I'm not?"

"What isn't pointless and drab?" she asked.

I shrugged and pushed my plate to the side. "Nothing, I guess. One thing isn't."

"What's that one thing?"

"I haven't found it yet."

She stuck a tuft of hair under the ribbon. "So what do you want, Harry?"

"I wanted to have breakfast with you," I said.

"You've already eaten and I'm not hungry. I told you how busy I am with the divorce and everything else."

"What everything else?"

"Everything else," she said.

"I keep forgetting you're married."

"So do I. That's why it didn't last too long."

"I'm wondering what I'm supposed to be doing with this."

She took a card from her purse and jotted something on the back.

"This is the address of the golf club where Ben worked,"

she said. "The manager is a slippery asshole named Montero. Maybe he can tell you something."

I looked at the card, back at her serious face. I yearned to say something, to straighten her out, but I got lost in her frown.

Sue said, "I have to be somewhere." She slipped out of the seat, her umbrella dripping rain onto the floor. "Thanks for the breakfast," she added.

"Let's do it again sometime."

She turned, then stopped. The gamblers were studying her studiously. "What do you really want?" she asked.

"I suppose I don't know. I suppose I'll tell you some day. I suppose I won't know then—just as well I don't now."

"You've got a sense of humor," she said. "Meet me at Clover's at six, six-thirty tonight and we can have a real talk, like people. With drinks and soft lighting."

After she left the gamblers grumbled and ordered coffee and one of them scooped the cards into his breast pocket. The game was over. One of the fellows jabbed a finger into the sleeping man's shoulder and he rose up, startled. Then he lay on his crossed forearms once again. As one of the gamblers was passing me, he paused and slapped his palm amiably on my table. His eyes were opening and closing slowly, regularly.

Talking fondly he said, "That's some dame, huh?"

"Yeah," I said. "She is some dame."

"You can always tell," he said.

"Tell what?"

"What kind they are."

"What kind is she?" I asked him.

His head twitched. "That one I can't really tell," he said.

I agreed with him.

I arrived at the country club, where Bergen had been employed, at around 11:30, my stomach heaving with the six or seven cups of bad coffee I'd downed at the restaurant. The receptionist was a priggish woman in white pants and shirt, with a bad case of glowering. She told me that I could wait while she inquired after Mr. Montero, the starch fairly discernible on the edge of her tongue.

"Mr. Montero might very well be preoccupied," she said.

"I'll wait for him."

"Who shall I tell him is waiting?"

"Jome," I said. "Just inform Mr. Montero that it's about an employee of his. If you don't mind."

"Of course I don't," she said.

"That's good of you."

The club's lobby was posh and decorated with veiny plants that touched the ceiling, a few cigar boxes with tees, five or six bright caps. I sauntered around a minute while the receptionist went into the back. Another man was seated alone at a card table, staring ahead as though in the throes of a remarkable dope addiction. Dull jazz peppered out of invisible speakers and struck the brown and burgundy walls. I felt flattered just to be in the rich cigar fumes the club exuded. Outside, some laughing men were spinning manically around in golf carts, carousing through puddles and getting soaked. I didn't understand the appeal. But to be fair, I didn't understand the appeal of anything, really.

Montero was lean and tan and had long arms. He came out from a back room of blue lockers and coat racks and grinned as though he meant every inch of it. He was dressed like the other golfers who'd been passing chattily by—khakis, floppy cartoon hat, white spiked shoes—but his attire was slimmer, the kind of fit that makes you want to snap your fingers rhythmically. I guessed he was sixty years old.

There was a moment of hesitation after the receptionist pointed me out.

"Mr. Jove," he said, jerking his hand toward me. His accent was strange and I couldn't quite place it.

"Jome," I said.

"Yes."

Montero's grin eloped from his eyes when he glanced at the vacant man at the card table.

"That's Corvis," the manager said in a whisper. "He cannot be communicated with when he goes into these trances of his. Occasionally he is incapacitated for an entire two days, and we sometimes have to simply leave him when we close at seven. His wife is dead and that may have something to do with his condition. Still, it is unfortunate and we are hopeful," here Montero lifted his eyebrows, "that Mr. Corvis will find another location to do his fretting."

Montero had an uncluttered way of talking. English was doubtlessly his third or fourth language, and he went about trying to prove that it could be good enough even for him.

I followed him into the rear of the club, where several wealthy men were lounging with their backs against the wall, exchanging inane anecdotes that were about as humorous as nicotine. Those same gigantic plants were sprouting everywhere.

"What's with the forestry?" I asked.

"To oxygenate. Better for the health of our members. I'm glad you appreciate our botanics. I bred them myself."

"Must have been uncomfortable."

He smiled tightly at me over his shoulder, the joke lost or not very funny or both.

His office was equal parts dingy and anachronistic. Ill-lit, stained glass lamps suffused the niche in partitions of uneasy light, as though the room had been specifically graphed to provide the least amount of illumination. An extravagantly red desk, bare except for an expensive fountain pen and a box of notecards, separated us. Montero slapped a pair of white gloves on his thigh and placed them gingerly off to the side of the desk. I could smell that it was nice wood.

"I collect Tiffany lamps," Montero said as I contorted into a high-backed chair. "That chair that you are sitting in was designed by William Morris. Do you know William Morris?" Montero looked at me thoughtfully. "And this *table*—I'm terribly sorry, but please do not touch your hands on it, thank you, Mr. Jove—this table belonged to William James, who was apparently fond of sniffing at the variegated odors of the oak. Do you like it somewhat?" He nodded at me for approval and kept nodding until I approved.

"It's fine as far as William James's desks go. I'm here about Ben Bergen," I said. "One of your former instructors."

Three unique alterations of a scowl fleetingly tugged at his thin, tan face. "If I remember correctly he was not a gifted player," Montero said. "But he was an erudite teacher, if I may so use that term."

"Use whatever term you like. What I'm most interested in is Mr. Bergen's psychological state toward the end of his job here."

"And why is Benjamin curious to you?"

"He killed himself and now his sister wants to know why."

Montero was put off by my bluntness and partly scoffed. "I didn't know," he said. "Ben is dead?"

"Yeah," I said.

"Oh." His eyebrows twitched, but they'd been twitching since I got there.

"Well, Ben was a cordial fellow," Montero said. "I was not so acquainted with him to offer an evaluation of his character. He was a good teacher and that's all I needed to know. Ben, of course, had his intense bouts of silence near the culmination of his time here, and he would often not talk to any of the staff for days."

"Did he ever mention anything to you?"

"I remember that I was shocked when he offered his resignation. He said he was leaving the city for a while."

"He say why?"

"Not that I recall."

"Ever hear the name William Florence?" I asked.

Montero shook his head, then stopped shaking his head, and shook his head some more. "It does sound familiar."

"How familiar?"

"Vaguely familiar, but not so familiar, I'm afraid, Mr. Jove."

"Don't be afraid. And it's Jome. There must be something else. What else?"

"What else? Frankly, Mr. Jove, I have nothing to add but what I have already mentioned," Montero said. His brows lifted, and his eyes suddenly glinted in the semi-darkness. "I do have this." He pulled on the white gloves and slid a drawer back open. He held a four-by-six-inch frame up to his eyes and pondered it for a moment. When he handed it over I saw that it was a drawing, the same one adorning Mrs. Bergen's wall. "Perhaps this is something. Ben gave it to me quite a while ago, for my birthday. I can't fathom how it would help you, Mr. Jove, but it's really a nice piece, don't you think?"

I scanned the blurred contours of the gray and black orchard. There was no difference that I could see between the two copies.

"Who drew it?" I asked.

"I haven't an idea," Montero said, and I believed him. "I insist that you take it for your little investigation. Perhaps I will need a favor from you some day," he said, in the cadence of a schmuck feigning inner knowledge of the underworld.

"Perhaps you won't get it," I said. "I could be ungrateful."

"Ha ha," Montero said for the both of us, rising like a bird from a feeder. I put the drawing under my arm when I stood. Just to be radical I ran a forefinger over the surface of William James' desk and heard Montero gasp. In the ante-room the golfers were giggling at a joke a newcomer had just told. They looked at me and stopped giggling.

I took one glance at the clubhouse as I headed back to the street. The course beyond was little more than a flat green monotony interrupted with sand traps and carts—elegiac and quite foolish. I started walking with the rain tickling my neck. After five minutes a cab pulled to the side without me gesturing for it. I told the driver to take me downtown. Though he didn't appreciate me dripping all over his uphol-stery, we did have a lengthy and enterprising discussion on socioeconomics and the weather.

Late on Friday afternoon the cop from Sutter Falls accidentally took my call after I told the secretary that I was a local politician.

"This is Banes," the cop said, his voice dripping with nepotism.

"Everything all right?" I said.

"Yeah. Why?"

"Never mind. I'm Harry Jome and I'm a private investigator in the city."

The voice immediately roughened up.

"Why would you say you were something else? I don't see the sense in that."

I asked if the name Ben Bergen did anything for him.

"Not enough to pay the phone bill."

"William Florence, maybe?"

"Florence, yeah. That's my wife's name."

"Tell her I said hi."

"Tell her yourself, she's right here."

I gave Banes a minute to let the banter get out of his system.

"I'm calling about a suicide. Motel room in your jurisdiction. Fellow named Bergen. Checked in under the name of Florence."

"I know it. Guy had no ID. Checked in under William Florence. Suicide," the sergeant said with the tone of a blunt tool. "That all you called for?" he asked.

"You're pretty thorough," I said.

"If that's an insult you can go climb a pine tree. If it's a compliment, thanks, we all appreciate it."

"How's things up north?" I asked.

"Not too bad. A few minutes ago a couple of the boys brought in some coffee and I drank it."

"No doubts it was a suicide?"

"We talking about Florence, or Bergen or who?"

"Yeah, still."

The sergeant breathed heavily. "OK look, Jome, if there ain't nothing else we have some real things to do here. So get off my line, buddy."

"The maid was the first person in the room?"

"What's your name again?"

"Jome."

"What's your last name?"

"Still Jome."

"Jome, call the motel yourself and get the hell off this line. We have a big zero over here and there's other messes besides talking to you."

"What about Daddy Longtree? He in your jurisdiction?"

"What the hell kind of name is that?"

"British, I think, but I don't know why that should matter. Bergen was up there visiting him. Longtree Orchard."

"OK, Jome, OK," the sergeant said gently. "Ben Bergen. William Florence. Daddy Longfellow. Whoever. I'm serious. Now get off my goddamn line. You boys need to quit molesting us."

"You boys?"

"That fink Lewis-something. I don't like him and I don't especially like you and you can tell him I said that."

"What's this Lewis-something want?"

"Same thing as you. Same thing as everybody."

"And what's that?"

"What we don't have. We can't give you what we don't have."

"You got nothing, huh?" I asked.

"And lots of it. Right now I'm going to get you off my line for you."

He either fell asleep or hung up. I flipped open my notebook and was shocked to see its condition. First, I noticed the absence of my notes and the mangled tear at the head of the binding. The pages had been ripped out aggressively. I wasn't too upset, insofar as the information I had stored there was easy to replicate and not very demonstrative to someone unfamiliar with the people who made up the Longtree case.

The second revelation was an embellished business card, an eye peering through a split, billowy cloud. "Parker & Porter, Consultants" is what it said. There weren't any particulars, as in what they consulted in, nor an address or phone number. On the reverse of the card, in measly scribbling, was the blatant warning and observation: *Fuck You, Jome.* I really needed a lock on my door, or a brand-new profession.

I dialed another number.

"Cramm's Tailor Shop," the voice said.

"I need a suit, bad."

"OK, this is Cramm."

"And soon," I said.

"Stop by in the morning, say 9:30?"

"I'll put it on my calendar."

"Me too."

Clover's Bar was the kind of joint that had all but shut down without anyone noticing. Its entrance was off an alleyway adjacent to 19th Street, along a portico lined with the sick geometry of spent bottles of beer. The interior was washed in signed photographs of celebrities, all forged in the same hand and snowed with dust.

The jukebox off in a corner was on, playing a song about a cocaine fiend who can't find anywhere to get any more cocaine.

Sue Longtree was already drinking a whiskey sour amid the decay as I joined her in a booth. When the barman wearied of watching me motion at him, he came over sullenly and I ordered a soda water. Sue looked at me over the red and white straw in her glass. Near her elbow was a plaid wallet.

"I'm surprised to see you in a place like this," I said.

"It's one of the only spots I can go where I don't have to be around people like me."

I stretched out my hands. "I don't have much more for you that I didn't have this afternoon."

"I was hoping you'd have something for me," she said. "Something small, at least. What happened with Montero?"

"Nothing."

"Why're you being so coy?"

"Because."

It was so dim in our niche it was almost blurry. Sue was wearing a shade of lipstick that did not flatter her ordinary lips. She'd changed her clothes for a black V-neck sweater that was cut low and that didn't seem to cover anything beneath it. One sly nipple pressed at the wool fabric. The jewels in her necklace were disheartened in the meek light.

"Go ahead," she said. "I enjoy knowing where my money's gone."

"How's your husband?"

"Weak. Disgusting. Infantile."

"It's not healthy to be so infatuated." Soda water was

brought to me in a pint glass, carbonation hissing at me and spilling onto the table. "Well?" I said.

"It would be pretty outstanding if you told me what's going on with you. You seem mean. You said you wouldn't be mean to me anymore," she said.

"I never said that, and why'd you hire these people to search my office?"

One corner of her mouth twitched. "What people?" she asked. "What office?"

"Parker. Or Porter. Or both. I don't know. I wasn't there. And now somebody called Lewis something-or-other."

She bit into an ice cube. "I didn't hire anyone," she said.

"I'll argue with you."

"So argue."

"It's starting to seem odd that your brother used Florence's name. Montero said it rang a bell?"

"Before you said it wasn't odd."

"Now I'm saying different. Who's William Florence?"

"Well, Harry, you're the detective." She wiped her hands on the tablecloth. "I asked you to find out why Ben killed himself, and you're sitting there all glib, just twiddling your face at me."

"I don't know what else to do."

"There's no other meaning in this."

"Maybe."

Across the bar a man in a sharkskin suit pulled a chair out for a lady in a green sequined dress. Immediately they started squabbling and picking at the pretzels in front of them, the woman chuckling in a cruel way at the man.

Sue drained the whiskey in a rapid sip.

"You haven't had too many cases lately, huh?" she asked.

I shrugged subtly, implying *probably not, no*.

She spat an ice cube into the glass. "So?" she said. "So what? I'm paying you to find out what happened to Ben and you're just—"

"You already know what happened to him."

"—just twiddling your face at me. I know what happened to him. I don't know why and that's what you're for."

"There's something else," I said.

"If there's something else maybe you can tell me what it is."

"If I knew what it was I'd tell you."

A man in a blue sweater sidled up to the bar and leaned

into the barman's ear and went out. I'd seen the man before, in the same sweater, but Sue interrupted my recollection.

"What do you have on Ben?" she asked.

"I don't have anything. You want me to make something up?"

"That would be an improvement."

"You're cold."

"If my personality bothers you you can hand me back the load of money I gave you."

"All right," I said. "It's true that I don't have three nice things to say about you and right now I can't think of two of them."

She grinned, pleased, spinning her glass in circles on the table.

I wanted her green eyes and the flex of her jaw and that single nipple that jutted at me. She was the kind of woman who needed something to prevent her from thinking. Her slender arms were hairless, with thin fingers splayed out like claws. The supreme awfulness of the place settled in. I was yearning for her and she knew it and I had just found out.

"I'd kind of expected you to have this all wrapped up by now," she said.

"I'm going to check the public archives in the morning," I said.

"Why would you do that?" she asked.

"Why wouldn't I do that?"

I stood and the barman stared me down as though I were ducking out on the tab.

"I'll get this one," Sue said.

"Good," I said. "I'll get the next one."

"The next one?" she said. "I really do think you like me."

"I haven't said otherwise. But this isn't really about who likes whom better."

Sue ordered another drink. "Have you ever heard the name Wald?" she said.

"Not really."

"He came by my house asking about you."

I fixed a quizzical look on her. "Why would this person do that?"

"I wouldn't ask you if I knew."

"You wouldn't tell me at all if you didn't know more than you're saying. What did he ask?"

"Where he could find you."

"And you told him you don't know."

"I told him where he could find you. He brought up William Florence. Said he was with the Bizby Agency."

"I'll look into it," I said.

I shimmied away from the table, leaving Sue to her whiskey and her condescension. On the way out I noticed Leo, the midget from the diner, unpacking his guitar case. He threw an enthusiastic nod at me, and I gave him one back. I was expecting the rain to have eased up but found that it had become clamorous, smacking the cement with the sound of one continuous explosion.

The name Wald didn't ring any bells. I didn't think I'd ever heard of him. What did he want with Sue? How did he know about her, or about me for that matter? I wasn't quite sure what to figure on.

I stayed out of the rain for a minute, sheltered underneath a busted neon sign. I peeked into the window and saw that Sue was still smiling at me from inside, a tight, lascivious smile that prodded me in the trousers.

B ack when I was a fresh, eager kid I spent weekends at the 6th Street Library, poring over Aquinas and the other deadly serious boys, the plague, the buying of indulgences, murderous kingdoms, fiefdoms and all the rest of that drab stuff. It was there that I'd met Wilma Baxter, a short, pallid girl with long bangs and straightforward eyes. For a librarian she was rather boozy and flippant and we went a few rounds but it didn't amount to much of anything. I hoped she still worked there.

The library was a graystone, Brutalist slab that stretched the length of the entire block. Several stuffed-looking employees attempted to show me to the newsprint section of the archives, where reading machines buzzed tiredly. I stooped at the information desk amid a huddle of zealous amateur historians all vying for the big hunch, and requested some editions of the local paper that would include the name Longtree. The clerk was afraid, he said, that the information was privileged, and he actually seemed afraid. He was lanky and he was looking at me like I should have been wearing a tie and a cravat.

"I was testing you," I said. "Get me Wilma, will you?"

"Is Ms. Baxter expecting you?"

"Well, we had sex a few times."

"Pardon me?"

"That's a good idea."

The guy fumbled for the intercom and paged the woman, his voice cracking like glass.

Wilma had become even more of a sardonic woman, only now she was a few years older and didn't care half so much about appealing to everyone as she did in school.

"Nice of you to come by just to see me, Harry," she said in a tone that, were it a color, would have been copper.

"You come in handy now and then," I said as she took my arm and led me to an uninhabited reading table in a corner where the shadows lurked. She was in a dark pencil-skirt, and her figure cut into the skirt, emphasizing how broad her hips had grown. Her bleached blond hair was brushed straight back, and there were creases at the corners of her mouth from smirking too much at idiots.

"After all," I continued, "you do fancy yourself in love with me and you always have. Ever since back then."

"There's a lot of love in the world and you are a very slim part of it," she said. Books were piled all over the table, spilling onto other bindings.

We sat quite close across from each other and stared. Her perfume was so strong I felt like it had been sprayed in my face.

"You look pretty different, Harry," she said, her eyes fixated on my mouth.

"I didn't mean to startle you," I said.

"You didn't startle me is what I'm telling you. Different is good."

"I thought different was bad."

"It depends on what you mean by *different*. And, I guess," she said, taking one of my hands, "what you mean by *bad*."

I felt her touch in my ankles.

"Remember all those winters?" she said.

"Could you get some stuff for me?" I said.

Wilma loosened her grip. "Oh," she said. "What would you do for it?"

Someone in a blue sweater flashed by and started looking at the titles on a shelf nearby.

"I'd be awful nice to you."

"Anyone can be nice to me," she said.

"Then I'll be rude."

"You are rude," she said. "But I like you and I like thinking that sometimes you might think about me and take me to an expensive dinner, for example."

"I don't think about you and I won't take you to dinner."

"You're romantic, kind of," she said. "And dumb. But honest."

She ushered me into a room the size of a phone booth laid on its side and sat glaring at a screen of microscopic type.

"What do you need?" she asked.

"Anything with the name Longtree stamped on it," I said.

Wilma kissed the back of my neck and went away when I told her to go away. Twenty minutes later she returned with some clippings in an overstuffed folder.

"Just don't take the originals with you, huh?" she said.

"You might lose your job for this," I said.

"Not when I'm married to the head librarian as of last Tuesday."

"Lucky girl," I said, patting her waist.

"Lucky guy," she said.

The work was tedious. Every once in a while I surveyed the slow bustle of scholars in the rooms beyond.

Daddy Longtree's folks were devout Methodists, the founders of Longtree Orchard, and also of a colonial inn on the grounds that had been quaintly dubbed Longtree Manor, but since then had been torn down to make room for more trees. Asked by a newspaperman why he had come to this country to start an orchard business, Simon Longtree responded, in that folksy eloquence of the period, that he couldn't have achieved much else with a name like his.

The article, a tribute to the Longtrees, was written 20 years after the events and printed in a bland Sutter Falls newspaper. Around that time the Longtree business was shipping apples all over North America and considering whether or not to export to Europe. They decided that they would not export to Europe.

Simon and his wife Margaret were discovered in a suite at the inn by a gardener who'd come asking about his paycheck. Margaret was on the floor in her nightdress, a knife sticking out of her stomach. Her husband had drowned in the bathtub—there was an inconsequential bump on the back of his head from the soap holder. The fall hadn't knocked him out and, it seemed, Simon Longtree drowned fully alert.

But it was the conclusion to the report that struck me: "The various tragedies meted upon the Longtree relations appear to have reached a bitter—yet considering later events—not more bizarre crescendo."

When I was finished with the article I searched for a William Florence in the city directory. There were two leads, the first living on 24th Street, the second a business address on 2nd. Browsing through a pamphlet-sized census I learned that Sutter Falls did not claim a resident with Florence's name.

I took away several photocopies of the juicy material from the rest of the Longtree files. Wilma wasn't at the information desk, but I didn't feel much like waiting to exchange more libidinous awkwardness with her and stepped out onto the massive library steps.

Rain stuttered on the cab's roof as I advised the driver how to make egg salad. Getting out of the vehicle at my apartment, rain pummeling the sidewalk, the city was condensed into a gray, melodramatic lingering place.

After the library I went to the tailor's. What I needed was a suit and a good one. Nice gray seersucker with a single-breasted coat and a matching vest.

By the time I was being fitted for a pricey three-piece at Cramm's little basement haberdasher's I was jubilant. I hadn't bought a suit in a while. The tailor didn't seem as excited as I was. He was a grim-eyed, balding man with pursed lips and a fraudulent smirk that wavered at the least provocation. He used the measuring tape to get my dimensions, jotting notes on the back of his hand. Once in a while he said, "Um," like he was surprised or puzzled.

I put half down.

"I'm not usually open on Saturday," he said at the counter.

"Me neither," I said.

"And I do not work on Sundays."

I asked, "Are there any days you do work?"

He shrugged sullenly, making the shrug look like a lot of work.

"Monday, maybe. We have a lot of orders at the moment. I can't promise anything."

"How about quicker than that?" I asked. "This suit's pretty important."

"I can't promise anything," he said.

"Like I said, it's pretty important."

"Like I said, I can't promise anything."

I paid him an extra $5 but he still looked uncertain, so I left, suddenly sour. Late afternoon had brought stronger rains, and sorry clouds roiled and swept by. I found a restaurant uptown and played with the salt and pepper shakers awhile. The waitress was puffy and liquored. I ordered a cheese sandwich on rye and a glass of milk.

Who cared that some guy had offed himself in one of those moments of weakness meant for the stage? Why a woman like Sue, who had the scruples of a hungry fish, would go through the trouble of hiring a private detective for this didn't register anything reasonable. Maybe there was more to it. Maybe she was just daffy, like the rest of them — Bergen's wife a drunk, father a hermit, and Sue too crazy for good sense. So the Longtrees were a nuclear collection of sociopaths and suicidal agrarians. To me it was as empty as a wedding vow, but I was being paid — thinking about it was directly against my own interests, whatever my interests were aside from the money in my freezer.

In any case, I was high about the new suit, in spite of the rain.

I poked around the newspaper for a minute while the waitress kept nudging the receipt closer to me.

Back at the office I rang some contacts in the journalism racket and found out that Parker & Porter Consulting was a legitimate operation, at least on paper. Also that their offices were at 301 East 51st Street, a depleted junkyard section of town. I eased myself out of the office and into a cab. The windows were fogged and I wiped my finger into the condensation until the cabbie told me to quit soiling his vehicle.

51st Street was drenched in the quietness of all drenched neighborhoods, but the kind of crouched hush that can get loud in a hurry. The trash bins were excessive and over-flowed with water, the cops were nowhere, a few residents wandered back and forth on broken porches. They were all black and white and frustrated.

Number 301 had a row of busted windows. A dirt path led to a sheet of plywood that doubled as an entrance. Two orange and white signs warned me that trespassers would not be tolerated. I had to hop onto the sloped porch from the ground. I pounded on the door and heard nothing but the porch dislodging under my feet. Radio news rehashed the events of the world from somewhere close by.

"Vacant," someone said behind me.

An old woman in a bonnet and white flats was staring at me when I turned, going back and forth frenziedly in a rock-ing chair on the next porch over.

"You know if someone was here a while ago?" I asked nice. "Two guys maybe?"

"Vacant," was all she said.

I said thanks and started down the destroyed steps. Halfway down the steps I pivoted abruptly and kicked the weakened door off its bottom hinge, and slipped inside the place. I stood silently for a minute, watching the spray of wood as it fluttered to the floor. There wasn't much to the place except for a roll-top desk and a moldy tea bag on top of the desk. I took a step in and paused.

Relieved of its rungs, a warped wooden ladder was propped on the wall, alongside a few dozen boxes with paperwork spilling out. I was cocky about breaking through a door for the first time and took a couple of footfalls into a wreck of pink insulation flowering around me and a collapsing ceiling, went over and grabbed a handful of papers from the boxes, reading contracts from cases and the occasional tax form.

Whoever he was, the guy sprang on me fast from my periphery. Then there was a scuffle as he wrapped my arm behind me to pin me against the wall, a beard tickling my spine, and he had me by the neck tight in the crook of a muscle. It happened so quick my first response was to laugh, and I gave one long chortle before I couldn't laugh anymore and didn't want to and he was laughing too.

"Hi," the bearded man said casually into my ear with a blast of disenfranchised breath.

He pushed me farther into the room, paused my strangulation and forced me to kneel. The place was a shambles, the floor stripped to the plywood foundation and strewn with nails and screws and bits of trash fluttering in through a gaping hole in the east wall.

"Hi," he repeated.

"Look," I said when he released me, finding some fear to put in my voice. "I just bought a fetching suit and I'd like to be able to wear it if you don't mind. I am trespassing, but I'm trespassing for a reason."

"Yeah," he garbled. "Yeah. Uh yeah," and then, finality lacing his words, "OK. So? So what?" His intonation was freakish, like he'd been taken over by an untuned radio station.

I couldn't be sure if he was armed or encyclopedically reckless. Turning slightly, I saw that my attacker was carefully biting the skin on his thumb, and not paying me any attention. He was nothing but a deadbeat with long, sand-colored hair that knotted at the top of his wide head. Additionally, he was completely naked, covered in filth.

"You squat here?" I asked. "Or is it your birthday?"

"I don't know, man. It is what it looks like."

He'd forgotten all about me. Extraordinarily blue eyes snapped suddenly and there was kindness in them, but not a lot of kindness. He dropped cross-legged onto a pile of stained rugs, rubbing his knees for warmth.

"Hey," he said. "So yeah. Yeah? Uhh, yeah. OK. So what? What is it? You going to judge, so judge me." He looked around frantically, rubbing his arms. "Where the hell my goddamn clothes go?"

"I'm wondering if some people stop by here?" I asked.

"Hey," he told me.

"We already went through that."

"Tomorrow," he said.

"Tomorrow what?"

"Tomorrow it will be."

"Not today though?"

He shook his head slowly.

"Are you sure?"

"Don't I fucking look it?"

"More than most." I thrust some dollar bills at him and brushed the debris off my pants.

"That's money," he said, taking it and sniffing the paper.

"Who comes by here?" I asked.

"Sure, two guys. They get the mail and right off. They don't say hello or anything. Just get the mail and right off."

"Is one of them fat and bald and shady."

Considering the image for five seconds, he narrowed his eyes and ran a hand through his knotted hair and then narrowed his eyes some more. "Yeah. And so is the other one."

"Who else? A mean redheaded woman?"

"I'd like her a lot," he said. "Bring her around if you can."

I started to leave.

"Guy named Lewishom," he said.

"What about a guy named Lewishom?"

"He came by and asked about the two guys who get their mail here."

"What's Lewishom look like?"

"Like ordinary. Blue sweater. Jacket. Head. Said he was a private eye."

"What was he asking exactly?"

"About the two guys who get their mail here, and he told me to tell them he hangs around at a billiards hall."

"Which one? Daim's?"

"Sure."

"How about somebody named Wald?"

"No," the guy said thoughtfully. "But I know guys by other names."

"What kind of other names?"

"You wouldn't know them, they're not named Wald. Oh wait," he said. "Wald, Wald. That sounds familiar."

"Keep it moving," I said. "Maybe you'll pick up some lint with it."

"No," he said. "I was wrong. It don't sound familiar very much."

I tossed him another ten. "Buy yourself some pants."

"This ain't enough for pants, you crazy?"

"Start with the cuffs."

I had another useless lead to go by, another big squeeze from all sides. Going from 51st Street back downtown was a short, wet journey, reduced to looking at the hint of a defunct metropolis. I passed a heap of cars and junked televisions in a fenced-in yard. Inside the perimeter men were rooting for objects of value. Stained glass windows flickered at me from the white church on 46th Street, the sole business in the area that was still rolling high. On 34th Street there was the old train station, now a megalith of jagged panes of glass, a gouged exterior, one railcar out front for nostalgic reasons that had been forgotten long ago.

Goddamnit.

I kept on. The rain was flooding into my shoes, and the instant I was back downtown I went into a loud department store and bought myself a new pair of shining wingtips.

"What do you think about that?" I asked the clerk.

"About what, sir?" the clerk asked sleepily.

"These new shoes."

"They're good. If we sell them they're good."

"You bet they are."

That night I stayed up till about four, polishing my
wingtips. At some point I must have drifted off, because
when I awoke the television was off and a shoe was in my
lap. Across the room, sitting in a chair I'd never seen before,
was the midget from the diner, Leo, his guitar case beside
him.

"Morning," he said.

"Is it. This a dream?"

"I wouldn't know anything about that," Leo said.

"It's a kicker if it is." I resumed polishing.

"Yeah, I guess it is. I don't know. I wish this rain would
quit it." He put his knuckles to his jaw in deep thought.

"Say," he said. "Maybe I'm dreaming you. You think of
that?"

"Sure. That would be neat."

Leo rubbed his face. I closed my eyes.

"I need a shave bad," he said.

"Where'd you get that chair?" I asked.

"Borrowed it."

I awoke in my bed a couple hours later, expecting Leo to
still be there. He wasn't.

It was Saturday and I spent the a.m. hours in my bathtub
scouring old documents for any mention of the Longtree
family, some photocopies of clippings, features and the rare
photograph of men with beards in breeches and frigid
women in billowing dresses. I perused back to the beginning.
From what I could gather, the story went something like this:

In the mid-1800s they'd come over from Scotland, settled
up north and didn't budge from the area. Langley Longtree,
Daddy's great-great grandfather, was convicted of slaughter-
ing his butcher in the old country and fled to America, dis-
graced but anonymous for a brief time. Apparently, Langley
unsuccessfully tried to do away with some more people and
eventually strangled himself in prison with his silk handkerchief. Daddy's great grandfather, Gregory Longtree, tended

the orchard and disappeared after a gruesome lynching of the mayor's wife during a holiday weekend around 1900.

The narrative was as obvious as a madhouse frenzy, like something worse than the plot of a gothic romance by someone who didn't like people, or cogency, very much. It was a crazy story that included disappearances, reappearances of key figures, darkness and havoc.

As far as Daddy Longtree's father was concerned, the only son among a legion of daughters, there wasn't much. He built the orchard into profit and lived in relative peace until the double suicide at the inn. The daughters, however, pretty much wandered the orchard and eventually dropped off the record. History doesn't generally notice those who don't attempt to magnify it. The violence in the family didn't take me aback; even in Sue Longtree there was something primitive and dreadful and cold. She was an arrogant mystery and there was no solution to her, just as there was none to her ancestors. I couldn't understand it.

I mulled over the Longtrees for about an hour, accompanied by a sloppy cello sonata by a German romantic who'd obviously had his heart broken continuously.

The sound of the rain was growing obnoxious. The tailor called to tell me that the suit might not be ready on Monday. And there was no chance it would be done before that. I was depressed about it but Cramm didn't seem to care.

I showered and cursed my tailor while I examined the contents of my closet. Toweling off I passed the window and happened to notice Parker in the courtyard, shaded by a poplar and talking to a fat companion, whom I guessed must have been Porter. Another man was a few yards behind them without an umbrella. Parker pointed out my apartment to his partner.

Going out the back I walked to the Bizby Detective Agency. It was a split-level suite of offices that signaled the very end of 34th Street, over by the swelling banks of the river.

I had no idea it could rain so much. Twigs and kids' toys and cans floated down the street. The agency was in an old factory that used to manufacture rubber bands. Now the grounds were treeless and not a slip of foliage was visible.

Inside, the expansive single room was spartan, and off to both sides were labyrinthine corridors. Serious men in hats with files tucked under their arms roamed in and out of the corridors, an atmosphere hectic and mechanical, as though everybody had been spat out of a machine.

I was forwarded by a harried secretary to a cubicle in the middle of the main room of small desks, where a bluff of a woman in a brown wool suit was sitting with a file open in front of her. She had her head lowered but strained lusty masculine eyes to look up at me. "I handle the men," she said, crumpling the folder and delivering it to the wastebasket under the desk as though it were a ritual. "If you seek consulting."

All around us typists hammered on keys with a sound as deafening as a catastrophic hailstorm. Occasionally all the typewriters would stop at once, and the woman would listen distantly and a little angrily until they resumed.

"One of these men you handle is someone I'm looking for," I said.

"Yes," she said. "Anyone in particular?"

"Wald."

The typewriters stopped again in unison and the silence lasted for about two seconds.

"Can I ask you what it's regarding?"

"Uh huh."

She didn't want in on the joke, but after awhile she said, "What's it regarding?"

"I was hoping you could tell me what he's working on so I would feel better about him bothering a case I'm on."

"That's not something I can do."

"Who's the supervisor here?"

"I am. I hand out the cases based on our consultants' abilities and do all the follow-up work."

"You're Bizby?"

"No," she said. "You a private dick?"

"Sometimes."

"We need more private dicks here. The workload is a nightmare."

"Why can't you tell me about Wald."

"Walter Wald," she said to herself. "Nothing I can tell you. We have strict policies."

"I bet you can tell me more than that."

"We have strict policies," she said, opening a file. "Didn't I mention that?"

"It really is crucial," I said.

"Is there anything else I can do for you?" she asked.

"You must have something," I said. "As one person in this rotten business to another."

"Oh, I have a lots," she said, her voice and face in monotone. Over the sound of the typewriters I had to lean close to hear what she was saying and it didn't help that she was talking so low.

"The reason that I can't tell you anything about Walt Wald is also something else I can't tell you about," she said.

"I am really asking," I said. I smiled brightly, and whether it was because no one had smiled at her in a long time, or because she saw how artificial it was, she relented.

"Mr. Walter Wald is no longer employed by Bizby," she said.

She blinked and I blinked back at her.

"Two mornings ago," she went on, "he was just gone. His stuff was gone. And there was a vulgar note for me taped to his chair." The woman went on talking about the note and how rude it was and how lousy Wald was and how everybody complained that he couldn't close a case if it had a latch. "He was probably an alcoholic of some kind."

"Most are in this racket," I said.

"Everybody but the ones who won't admit it."

I stood. "It's too bad about Wald," I said.

"No it's not," she said.

I left through the sea of clattering, wondering what Wald was up to. Nobody so much as glanced at me.

I took an overpopulated bus north to 24th Street, where a William Florence resided. Parker and Porter hopped on at the rear of the bus and stood with their backs facing me next to a grimy fellow with a large book who kept insisting that they find a seat.

At the next stop, a guy in a blue sweater got on and went for the rear and sat adjacent to the grimy fellow with the large book. I recognized him. The bus was becoming some kind of hardboiled convention.

The address for William Florence was in a bland neighborhood with a grassy median running through it and one or two trees that looked like they'd just been stuck there for later use somewhere else. It was a middle-class limbo fighting hard to appear upper-class. The yards were square and zoned with short fences and uncared-for thorny bushes. Some kids with dirty knees were tossing around a rubber ball and a group of yellow dogs was watching them.

I tapped on the door of a little white house with lace curtains in the windows, a reclining chair on the porch and some spilled soil on the floorboards. Boxes of wine bottles were piled here and there.

The guy who answered the door stood behind a torn screen, feeble and in layers of bulky clothing. He was past 70 but well cared for. Meticulously combed gray hair, a gray mustache that wasn't dissimilar from a Civil War major's. Frosty air stirred in the house with the rattling of a second person on the premises and the sound of the local news.

"Yes?" he said, drawing out the word until it almost resembled another.

"William Florence?"

"Yes?" he said again.

"Do you know someone named Ben Bergen?"

"No, is he running for office or something?" The old man leaned on the doorframe and licked his mustache.

"Not really. He's dead."

"Why should I vote for him, then?"

"I'm asking if you've heard the name."

"I've heard it from you just now."

Something caught Florence's attention out in the street and his wrinkled face wrinkled some more. The kids had Parker and Porter surrounded. The two dicks were trying to remain incognito, but the kids were relentless and kept badgering them to catch their ball.

"This neighborhood," the old man said. "Never used to be like this."

"What did it used to be like?"

"Not like this. We used to have parades once a week." He waited for a response and went on, "I never said it was exciting. I'm just saying it never used to be like this."

"How about the name Longtree? That sound familiar to you?"

"You seem very confused," he said. "I already told your friend or whomever that I don't know the name Longtree."

"What friend?" I asked sharply.

"Man came here this morning asking about the things you're asking about. Don't you have a friend who came asking?"

"I don't have any friends."

"Maybe that's the problem. So who are you, young man?"

"I'm a private detective and—"

"Oh," he said jovially. "Like in those books? Those Dominic Early things."

"Just like those," I said.

"I didn't know there were people like in those things. I'm glad you stopped by because I wouldn't have known that."

And he slammed the door in my face.

Down the block the kids had dispersed into small delinquent cliques. Parker and Porter were pretending to be engrossed by an electrician fixing a telephone pole. The electrician appeared irritated by them.

Who'd been asking about the Longtrees? I asked myself, and I was about to start knocking again when another bus halted, aimed downtown and thankfully vacant, at the bus stop.

Hurrying to get on I abandoned Parker and Porter. Both men hustled to catch up, waving their arms at the bus driver, who paid them no attention whatsoever. Through the rear window I watched the portly men recede in their disappointment. Porter threw his hat on the ground and Parker picked it up and mashed it on his partner's head. They were so cute in their routine that they weren't even cute.

I wondered, not for the first time, whether I was as inept as they were in this Longtree debacle. I was missing something and Sue was holding out, but on what I could only conjecture.

Ten blocks from my office I got off the bus and ducked into what had to be the smallest diner in the world, even advertised itself as such. A guy in chef's whites was nose-deep in a magazine. I ordered a coffee at the register, paid, then stood at the window, where there was room for maybe four people. Down the countertop a man had his head resting in his hands, doing something close to weeping, if not weeping outright.

Behind me somebody said, "Let me get a coffee." I turned to the familiar tone. It was Leo and his guitar case. The chef ignored him.

"Believe that?" Leo said to me.

"Hey, can I get a coffee?"

Still, he went unacknowledged.

"Jesus Christ. Forget it."

When shouting didn't work Leo despondently joined me at the window.

"I can't believe that," he said.

"Have some of mine," I said.

"I don't want any anymore." Leo snapped his fingers. "You working?"

"Yeah."

"You look it."

"I always look that way."

Leo wrinkled his face at the manic rush of rain and people outside. "That rain, huh?"

"I got to go," I said. I left Leo more than a half a cup of coffee.

"Be careful," he said.

"What's the matter?"

"Probably nothing," he said. "Maybe everything."

Parker and Porter were waiting for me in the dilapidated gazebo outside my building. Sitting one on either side of a bench, both were in monochrome vests, sleeves rolled into sloppy bunches, suit coats folded in the empty space between them. I drifted over through a horizontal burst of rain.

When they saw me Parker stood up, trying to be menacing and cool. His partner had given up on anything more excessive than tilting his head. Water ran down both their faces, and I was discomfited by how closely they resembled one another.

"Jome," Parker said in his razor-blade-on-whipped-cream voice. "Sit with us a second, huh? What do you fucking say to that?"

"It might even be fascinating," his partner said.

I sheltered myself underneath the outer ring of the gazebo.

"You boys are as fascinating as ice cubes in a toilet."

Porter said, "That's fascinating actually."

"That you think it is proves my point."

Porter took the coats and set them on his lap and Parker and I sat. Three middle-aged guys sharing the silence of an existential dread. All we needed were bowler hats and canes and a box of caramel drops. Parker and Porter crowded against me.

Crisp leaves blew at our feet in a multicolored river.

"I brought my partner along," Parker said, "because we want to know something—"

"And maybe so do you," Porter said.

"This is my partner." Porter smelled like cheap aftershave after it's been worn by someone else. He was only about an inch shorter than Parker.

Porter pressed in tight to announce his toughness.

"Get him off my face," I said.

"What we'd like to know," Parker said. "Is what it is we aren't supposed to fucking know."

"What we don't know yet," Porter said. "What, in other

words, we aren't supposed to know?"

"But we are planning on knowing the facts," Parker said. "Such as what you're fucking doing with lady Longtree."

"Such as that," Porter said.

"The fucking facts, Jome."

I turned from one to the other of the private dicks, quickly evaluating the knowledge that they didn't know a single thing about a single thing.

"You two boys figure it out and I'll be right here if you need anything," I said.

"What stymies us," Porter said, "is what's going on with the Longtrees and you and stuff like that."

Parker said, "And we're going to be around you until we fucking find out."

"The lady has you looking at a suicide," Porter said.

"So what's so big about it?" Parker asked. "It ain't real interesting but you and she are acting like it's real fucking interesting. So why is it so interesting?"

"Yeah, why?" Porter said.

There was a little green park going brown across the street, and people in suits were hurrying around in the rain. Across from us on another bench was a man leaning our way, in full denim attire. A wind from the east blossomed and Porter clutched at the hat he'd thrown on the road a little while ago.

"Our affiliation is purely professional," Parker said.

"Only thing professional about either of you is your absence," I said. "And that's debatable."

Almost in unison they each took one of my arms in fat, quaking hands. "Listen, Jome," they said in a gravelly duet.

"Listen, Jome," Parker said for a second time. "This is fucking serious and we're fucking serious about it. Our employer would like to be kept abreast and our client is fuck-ing serious, too."

"I'm sure your client is serious. Everybody's serious."

"This isn't a routine," Porter said, taking off his hat and dumping rainwater out of the brim.

"You said you have some information for me." I brushed arms away, standing, and glared at them. "Where is it?"

"Well," Parker said. "Suppose, now just fucking suppose, that you throw us a scrap and we toss something back to you."

I jerked a finger at Porter. "Why's he so quiet all of a sudden?"

"Jome is funny," Parker said to his partner.

"He thinks he's funny," Porter said.

"Yeah, and he's not very funny."

"He's not very funny at all because he thinks he is."

A woman halted a dog to urinate in front of us and the woman blushed at the three of us and walked off.

"Fuck you," Porter said.

"I'm glad you're being yourself again," I said.

"You're not saying anything helpful," Parker said.

"How about this," Porter offered. "We'll tell you something helpful and then you can tell us something helpful about you and Sue Longtree.

I did my best impression of being impassive.

"All right?" Parker said.

Porter nodded. "Yeah, I think he might be OK with that."

"There's another guy on you," Parker said. "Has the name of Wald and this Wald is sitting right over there." He flicked his head toward the guy in jeans and jean jacket and smiled.

"Thanks," I said. "But that's recycled news."

"So what do you have for us?" Parker asked.

Porter said, "Because we've just given that to you."

"As a gift."

I adjusted my coat, which had been crinkled by their bulbous mitts. "Once I get the drift of something I'll be sure to let you know," I said. "See you fellows later."

"That's not very nice," one of them said.

"Not very nice at all," said the other.

When I hurried across the street and passed the man in denim, he quickly scurried to his feet and followed me along the sloshed avenue. I walked downtown with him glued on me, pausing whenever I paused. Around city hall he disappeared in a conglomerating crowd. Sure that he was gone, I doubled back and took a cab to Daim's Billiard Hall.

There were a few worthless characters there ensconced in the crosshatched shadows surrounding the nine or ten tables. Felt and leather pockets shone in the meager light, and the floors were scrubbed with blue chalk and talcum. Behind a glass-topped counter that wasn't filled with anything a grizzled guy in coveralls was trimming his beard with a little pair of scissors. He put the scissors down when he saw me and scowled.

I'd been inside Daim's three or four times for a couple of games on a job once, a minor marital squabble that netted a few dollars and not much else. Wes Daim, a stagnant guy in his mid-50s who had done nothing but grin constantly and look like he might implode at any moment from some inside joke. What impressed me about the place was the enigma of the farthest table in the rear. It was roped off and marked with a sign that read DO NOT TOUCH. Only four balls were on the table, the eight ball, a solid and a high stripe, all lined up against the same rail, with the cue near the center of the red felt. I'd asked Wes about the unfinished game and he had mumbled something about an interruption eight years ago, and had walked into the bathroom and come out red-eyed, not wearing the fake smile he had gone in wearing. I didn't pry anymore into it, nor had I been in there since.

Wes didn't own the joint anymore, and the guy in cover-alls was not nearly as friendly, or friendly at all.

"Someone named Lewishom comes around here," I said to him.

The guy pried some tape off the glass. "You came in here just to tell me that?"

"It was more like a question."

Out of the shadows a glum kid of eighteen or less sidled up to the bearded man with a pool stick. "Lewishom isn't here just now," the kid said.

"You have good ears," I said.

"Kid, for chrissakes, did you finish what you were doing?"

"I did everything," the kid said.

"You know Lewishom pretty well?" I asked him.

"Yeah, he's my uncle," the kid said.

"He ain't your uncle, kid."

"He's a good guy," the kid said. "I think he would wonder what you want."

"He would wonder that," the bearded man agreed.

"I need to tell him what I want."

Pool balls clanked together behind me, whispers coming from the back.

"He won't be back for a few days. He's away," the kid said.

"Where is he away?"

The kid and the beard glanced at one another.

"We'll tell him you stopped by," the beard said.

"Who should I tell him was looking for him?" the kid

asked.

"I'll tell him myself," I said. "Where do you suppose I can get to your uncle?"

The kid let his eyes wander over to the proprietor's and the bearded man gave a slight nod. "At the burlesque club," the kid said.

"For chrissakes, kid, you clean the bathroom?" the bearded man exploded.

"I told you I did everything."

"Then go do something else until there's something else to do."

"Which club?" I asked.

The bearded man said, condescendingly, which didn't seem to be his nature, "The only burlesque club in town."

The kid gave me an address on 27th Street, and I hustled over, soaking my ankles in a series of puddles as I ran.

The joint was called Shays Burlesque and would have been a good definition of chintz. Polished dance floor covered with tables and chairs, booth-lined walls with candles running the length of a built-in shelf, and a dark wood bar that could accommodate nine or ten individuals. Dangling above the bar was a chaotic fixture of jagged, translucent shards that filtered a reddish light onto the rows of lowbrow liquor. For all of its glitter Shays was the opposite of dazzling. Besides Lewishom, easily identified by his tattered blue sweater and sitting in a booth close to the stage, the place was deserted.

I pulled up a stool and sat at the bar, ordered a club soda from a bartender who was obviously drunk. "We used to have 12 girls doing five shows a night," he said, holding my five-dollar bill out and scrutinizing it. On his forearm a violin was tattooed.

"How many girls you got now?" I asked.

"Still 12. But it ain't the same."

"What's that symbolize?" I asked, pointing at the ink on his arm.

"A violin," he said, and went to the mirror and started disarranging the bottles there.

By the stage Lewishom was bent at his table; he pinched out the candle's flame in front of him, relit the candle with a lighter and snuffed it out again.

At five after five the show started. Twelve girls pranced onstage wearing black corsets and white stockings and garters. Their moves might have been burlesque, but they just looked disordered and tired. A stocky man to the right was beating on a piano and a tall blond fellow was behind, wearing a dumb expression, and slapping his upright bass like he'd had a long-standing grudge against the instrument. The whole thing was amateur, and the number just made me sadder than I could have ever been at the moment.

All the while Lewishom was twisting his head, apparently following one of the girls with his eyes. From where I sat I couldn't tell which one, and even if I could, the garish spotlight seemed to drain every girl of any personal features.

The show lasted a half hour with no break and the girls danced off the stage while the musicians struggled to finish the song.

Lewishom stood uncertainly and headed out a side door marked THIS IS NO EXIT. I went out the front. On my way the bartender raised his arm and showed me his tattoo again. I circled the building, grappled through a wet crowd and reached the alleyway. Lewishom was already talking to one of the girls while he shed the ash of a cigarette onto his shoe, and finally dropped the butt and stamped on it forcefully.

The girl was in a tan raincoat and I could see by her stockings that she hadn't changed after the act. She was olive-complexioned and plump, a red silk scarf on her head.

I crouched beside a dumpster, close enough that I could hear Lewishom's frantic talk and the girl's coolly supercilious replies.

"Must be cold in that," Lewishom said softly.

"What do you want, Sid?"

"To buy you a drink and take you somewhere warm."

"I already told you no. I tell you every night and you keep not listening. You're here every day."

"But you haven't told me no tonight yet."

A pause.

Lewishom continued. "I've never seen you in the daytime, you know that? I bet you look good over a plate of toast."

"You're creepy," she said after a minute. "I'm going to have a drink all right, just not with you. And I don't like toast."

"I've got some money and I'm going to leave her once this thing is taken care of."

"I don't want you to leave her; she'll be almost upset or

something. What kind of thing is that to do?"

"She's always almost upset. But I'm telling you, the second this thing is over we could travel away somewhere."

Silence.

"I don't understand," Lewishom said, much louder now. "How you can be so—"

"Because it's *fun*," she said and giggled.

"It's not fun for me."

"That's why it's fun for me."

All of a sudden I heard the door creak open and someone exit the club. A few distraught words ensued. The girl and the blond man wheeling a huge hard shell case went by me without noticing that I was there. She had the musician's arm.

Leaving my spot behind the stink of the dumpster I saw that Lewishom was still rooted to the spot, shaking the rain out of his cuffs and just looking miserable, illuminated by a spazzing bulb above the door. He looked at me and walked back inside the club without bothering to look at me again and I decided to let my questions drop for the moment.

I **was exhausted** all over but couldn't fall asleep till about five on Sunday morning, on the semicircular sofa in my living room. I was staring at the ceiling like it was etched with some of the answers I wasn't getting, falling into dumb dreams about childhood and snowfalls and Sue Longtree, waking every few seconds in a sweat. My dreams were taunting me. I dreamt of everything but it was all the same. I was ready, alert. Sounds that didn't bother me now bothered me. The quiet street beyond the window with the infrequent car horn. The off-kilter ticking of the clock. The interminable tapping of faucets competing for annoyance.

When I came out of the last menacing dream I was on the floor and Sue Longtree was bending over to shake me. I tried pinching the ceiling. Sue replaced a pillow that had tumbled off the sofa.

"Don't leave your door unlocked," she said. "Or people like me will wander in."

"What the hell do you want? I haven't been sleeping too well."

"Sure, I'll have a seat."

We sat next to each other on the sofa. I ironed the fatigue out of my eyes with my thumbs. I was morose and hot. "And so what do you want?"

"Nothing much. It's Sunday."

"What's so great about Sunday?"

I saw that she was wearing a nice-fitting pencil skirt, her lipstick hyper-realistic against the rest of the picture.

"I know you'll tell me how you found me," I said.

"A phone book."

"I'm not in one."

"Get me one, I'll show you."

"I can't afford luxuries."

"You can now."

"Now it's too late." I started to get up but she put a hand on my thigh, enough to quit thinking about getting up ever again.

"Too late for what?" she asked, digging around in her purse for a cigarette.

"All the numbers I need belong to people I don't. Mostly them, or their ex-wives or my ex-wives."

"Least they're in the plural."

"Most awful things are."

She tapped the cigarette on her knee. Her hair looked good. Indecent snapshots of her body kept me busy while she lit the cigarette: slim breasts, protruding bottom, a swath of pubic hair kept neat and trimmed like a railroad track. A gold Zippo flicked in her palm with a little ruby lodged in the side.

I crawled out of the gutter in my mind and said: "Anyway. What are you here for?"

"I'm here to have a conversation with you." She blew smoke off to the side. "What is it exactly that you do?" she asked.

"This."

"What else? Where'd you come from?"

"Well, I was young, and pretty soon I was older and what happened in between makes no sense to me and won't to you either. I studied medieval philosophy in college, learned just enough to twist any thought I could ever have, married twice and divorced twice. I spend at least three hours a day wishing I was doing something else than what I'm doing." I leaned closer to her and she didn't object. "I have a deep, almost religious disinterest in everything and the world treats me the same."

"You're interested in me, though."

Sue leaned in and I sniffed at her perfume.

"My interest is piqued," I said.

"I think something else is piqued too."

"I also get excited when I watch a tarantula in a glass cage."

"Is that what I remind you of?"

"No, but a tarantula in a glass cage always reminds me of you now."

She smoked in short, abrupt puffs, holding the cigarette close to her eyes.

"Does it?" she whispered.

"I think so," I said. "I forgot the question if there was one."

With the cigarette she was doing something more than smoking. The pursing of her lips and the strange eyes when she inhaled were about as distracting as a kid on a tractor.

She grinned weakly and stood, sliding on those fat sunglasses. It was the kind of face that would make you starve to death at a buffet.

"Then I'm afraid," she said curtly, "that I have an appointment somewhere. Why don't you want to come over tomorrow night?"

"You say it like you've already asked me. Will Parker and Porter be there?"

"Who're they?" she asked.

I grinned wide. "Nobody."

"You're so smart you're almost moronic. Pick me up at 7:30 tomorrow, and if you're late, I truly don't know what I'll do with myself. But a string quartet is playing and I'd rather not miss it. At least not the Schubert."

She dropped her cigarette into a glass of water on the coffeetable, watching it float there with obvious pleasure.

"I wouldn't have pegged you for a Schubert fan. More in the Wagner line. Somebody brassy and harsh."

"He's the only one I know," she said. "I don't have the energy for that kind of thing."

She fired up another cigarette while she was in the doorway.

"What do you have the energy for?" I asked.

"Nothing much," she said. "But I'm learning."

She lingered there, pouting at me.

"How did you find out about me, anyway?" I asked. I sat up a bit on the sofa, not taking my eyes off her for an instant. "I don't believe you about the phone book."

"I researched you some," she said.

"Am I very engrossing?"

Her answer was an ambiguous scrunch of the shoulders. "You've had some trouble, so I guess that makes you entangled. And sad is another of your tendencies. I've had trouble, too," she said, leaning on the doorframe. "So we're close, Harry."

"What did you find out about me?"

Sue spent the second cigarette, mashed it on the hallway floor, and put another in her mouth. This one she didn't ignite.

"Not much," she said. "Just a lot."

"There isn't a lot about me."

"There's enough to get a vague picture."

"But I don't like being photographed."

Sue looked beyond me. "You spent some months in an institution right after you finished college," she said, and her eyes found me, and there was glee in them, at how uneasy she was making me. "What were you in for?"

I got up and wiped some dust off the bookshelf.

"What were you in for?" she asked again.

I kept dusting, finally said, "I flailed when I got into the world. Some people flail, and I flailed and I didn't know what I was supposed to do. How'd you find out about that?"

She glossed over what I had said.

"And then you're a private investigator all of a sudden."

I didn't appreciate the way she was talking, but she hadn't said anything untrue.

"What happened in the madhouse?" she asked.

"Madness."

"See, that's why I hired you. Wasn't that your question? We're both a tad crazy." Sue was anxiously whirling the ciga-rette in her hand. "There's three kinds of people," she went on, watching the movement. "Those who need to be coddled; the ones who want to be pushed away; and lastly, the kind you aren't so sure about."

"Which one are you?" I asked.

"I'm not so sure."

"People like to make generalizations," I said.

"Like that?" she asked. There was a very faint, very cute dimple on her left cheek. Our gazes were fixed on each other.

"Just like that," I said.

Sue Longtree dropped her cigarette and walked a heel over it without having lit it. I swiped away another ball of dust and when I looked at the doorway the doorway was empty.

Out the window I watched her cross the courtyard. Her bright umbrella faded away, blurred by colorful awnings and vendor's carts.

I returned to the sofa and sat there till 10:30, so tired I wasn't tired in the least, wondering what I was going to wear that night and feeling bad that my suit wasn't ready yet.

I shaved diligently, nicking myself in several spots, threw

on a bit of aftershave. According to the mirror I was not looking grand. Now that I was moving around I was more tired than ever, in that hazy limbo between sleep and wakefulness that was quickly becoming for me a sustained present.

The rest of Sunday I floated around the apartment, wasting time cleaning, drinking coffee and talking to myself. I took a short walk in the rain, but I couldn't outpace the compulsion to see Sue Longtree. I missed her and it was peculiar, insofar as I didn't even like her very much.

Sunday evening had no sleep for me, and the rain was a score to my insomnia—propulsive, horrible, desperate. I tossed in bed until 5:15, flopping into a dream and back out with an irregular onrush of frenetic episodes, unsure whether they were dreams or fragments, indications of a new reality. I was down, and rather than simply picking myself up I was digging down farther.

I wasn't sure when I'd quit sleeping. The long minutes drooled by—sweating, crazy fierce things. I had no one to be upset with. Because I couldn't sleep I was also unable to wake.

I dragged myself out of bed and dressed. For some foolish reason I was expecting sunlight with dawn, chirping birds and all the rest. But the rain was perpetual.

Leo was pouring himself a thermos of coffee in my kitchen. His plaid jacket had a coffee stain on the collar.

"Harry," he said, screwing the top on his thermos.

I got myself a cup, drained it with a jerk of my head. I expected the midget not to be there with the first flurry of caffeine. But he was. I said bye and he gave a nod. In the living room I halted, halfway out the door. Montero's gift, the orchard drawing, was hanging above the television. A little footstool was off to the side.

"Hey, Leo?" I called out. "You do this?"

Silence came at me from the kitchen. I shook my head, closed the door behind me.

The city had the veneer of polished bronze and the dirty streets were becoming less populous, fog and rain determining the shapes of landmarks. I was levitating alone in an elevator that blew dull music and belonged to another William

Florence.

On the 29th floor the doors clicked and parted and I was standing in a reception room of the Allied Insurance Company. The outfit controlled the whole floor, and the waiting area was shiny and transparent; some designer had gone to a lot of trouble to make the place as uninviting as possible. Shards of jagged white glass hung from the ceiling, providing a glow to select areas of the waiting room. The furniture looked like a woodworker's rudimentary diagram of furniture. All in all the place was nothing but perfect lines and zero decoration.

Behind a modernist desk a pouting secretary with too much indifference and a neat bob in her brown hair was polishing her wedding ring with a tiny scrap of cotton.

"I'm here to speak with William Florence," I said.

"He's not here," she said, continuing to scrub.

"OK, he's gone for the day?"

"You could say that," she said.

"I just did, and you're being cryptic, miss."

"Look," and her eyes swept over me quickly. "He's not here. Is there something I can do about his not being here?"

"There is, but it's not a nice thing to say to a woman."

She seemed to enjoy being insulted and smiled wanly at me with a big, white mouth, and stuck the wedding band on her index finger. Before pushing at the intercom button she was already talking into it.

"Mr. Perle. Someone for Mr. Florence is here."

In another room a man's subdued voice calmly replied from two places at once. "Is this gentleman a client?"

She looked at me questioningly. I nodded and winked at her and she nodded and winked back.

"I'm not sure what he is, Mr. Perle. Seems to be implying that he is."

"One minute," the man said. "No. Two minutes."

"This Perle is very particular," I said, checking my watch.

"Mr. Perle is very particular."

"You can sit over there," she said without specifying where.

I stuck my hands in my trouser pockets and circuited the room. Diplomas were archly displayed on the dark walls like carcasses in a butcher shop. Photos of company parties and outings attached with rectangular captions explaining where they were taken and who was in the picture.

Laguna Beach. Mr and Mrs. Fred Schiller on a twin paddle boat.

Juneau. Mr. Perle and Mr. Freely enjoy a discussion and a schnapps aboard the *Scuttlefish*.

Toronto. Mr. Shumley, McDaniels and Peterman at the top of the CN Tower.

Next to these ostentatious examples was a list of organizations that had benefited from Allied's money-grubbing. A few feet down the wall, frames bearing senators and actors embracing Allied spokespeople and executives in warm poses.

In most of the pictures where he appeared, Perle was a rather sallow, sable-haired man keen on anonymity, unaware that he was being photographed.

The intercom crackled.

"Tell him to come in," Perle said.

"You can go in," the secretary said.

"Thanks, you've been real swell about it," I said.

I stepped through a tinted glass door the secretary held back for me.

"First door on the left," she murmured and withdrew.

I didn't knock.

Perle's office was expansive and burgundy and neat. Expressionist paintings lined the wall without any distinction of style or color-scheme. Perle was sitting forward on a leather settee, his serious, uncompromising face following me across the room. Wire-rimmed spectacles sat on the top of his gray-tinged head. The nickel railheads of the settee shone fantastically in the track lights. Perle's hands were pure white, and the tight-fitting tan suit he wore was so well pressed he looked unclothed.

"I appreciate you seeing me," I said.

Perle's solemn face didn't do anything.

"How's the insurance business?" I asked.

He stirred finally, and when it dawned on him that he might have to speak, he said in a clean voice: "The insurance business has been doing remarkably well throughout history." He studied my rainy shoes. "Are you a client of ours?"

"Not in the technical sense."

"Then in what sense, please?"

"I'm a private investigator and I'm looking into the

Longtree family. Ben Bergen specifically. Know him? And your partner or whatever he is keeps coming up in polite conversations."

Perle's expression was as undemonstrative as a sack full of drab neckties. "Is there a question in that babble?" he asked. He looked at the clock on his desk. "You have four minutes and you can begin with a name."

"It's Jome and I'm wondering if a man named Florence is around."

Perle rose from the settee and leisurely made his way to the desk and snapped open a briefcase.

"He used to work for us. Bill was one of our consultants."

"What happened?"

"He doesn't work here anymore."

"So what happened?"

Perle squinted deeply.

"Let's just say he doesn't work here anymore."

"All right. He doesn't work here anymore. Why?"

"Mr. Jome, I believe you mentioned someone else's name that you are investigating. How is Bill involved in that?"

"Bergen used Florence's name."

"What did this Bergen do? Did he rob a laundromat?" Perle grinned wolfishly, as though he'd just brought an audience to its knees.

"I don't know why Bergen would have used Florence's name unless they were close. Is Florence working on some assignment?"

"You have one minute," Perle said, this time not even consulting the clock for verification. He stuffed some papers into the briefcase and latched it.

"Why won't you tell me about Florence? What's the trouble?"

"In the insurance business it's best that our customers know they're safe with Allied. It wouldn't do if—"

"What?"

"You are intruding and now since I have allowed my time to be wasted, I'm going to waste your time for a minute, Mr. Jome. Do you have insurance? Everybody in the world needs insurance."

Satisfied with himself, Perle slipped into a raincoat, grabbing the briefcase off the desk.

"Nobody told you?" he asked.

"Told me what?"

"That everything is a game. And if you don't know that, Mr. Jome, then you obviously aren't winning. It surprises me no one told you that."

"Maybe I heard it when I was researching a paper called 'How to be an Asshole.'"

Perle's tight mouth tightened some more. "I like the way you are," he said.

"And I like the things you say. Thanks. You're not going to tell me anything about Florence, are you?"

"I'm not," he said.

I was reaching for the door when I spotted it, mixed in with the other artwork. It was that same drawing of the orchard, the one from the Bergen place and the one hanging in my apartment that Montero had given me. All the lines and sloppiness of the thing were identical; it was unsigned.

"Who did that one?" I asked as Perle studied me studying the drawing.

"I have no idea."

"It's on your wall."

"So it is. I see what you mean. I would consider selling to you."

"I already got one."

"Then I hope you have a fine day with yourself."

I went back through the secretary's station. The girl was still polishing her wedding ring.

"Get some black tea and a bottle of 90 percent," I said.

"Does that get tarnish off?"

"No. But it might take the edge off you."

Back in my office I immediately phoned my tailor.

"Cramm," he said.

"Is it done?" I snapped over the line, right in the space where most people say hello.

"No," he said. "Who's this?"

"Jome."

"I know," he said. He took a moment to collect his response.

"I've gotten backed up," he said.

"How backed up?"

"Pretty far backed up."

"You aren't a good tailor," I said.

"I never said—"

I slammed the phone down.

The taxi I called for was late in coming and dropped me at the corner of 3rd and 4th at around 8:15, right by a defunct flower shop whose roses and sunflowers and poppies were rotting in their planters out front. When the cab pulled away another cab drew up and a man gazed out and quickly turned away. His cab was followed by a green sedan with its lights on. I noticed this because the guy in the cab had his window down, and I heard him say in an urgent voice, "Keep going. Just keep going."

I crossed the intersection and went up the cobblestone walkway. I was wearing a natty black raincoat and spats, but the rain had lessened to a dull patter.

Sue's place was close to the street, and brick and mortar all the way up to a blue shingled roof, quaint chimney—utilitarian and imposing. Some thick bushes obscured the windows on the side and I could just make out a corner of the swimming pool, lying on which was a tarp currently being slapped at by raindrops. For a raw second the moon glimmered noncommittally and then didn't glimmer anymore and the rain shunted harshly off the eaves. Two sleek cars were parked in the drive, one a wine-colored Peugeot, the other a Jaguar with mud on the rims and bumpers.

I stood on the shag mat and clanged the brass knocker, shaped like a huge ring in the nose of a rusted frog.

Almost immediately the door was pulled back by a wiry, grim-faced man on his way out. He was entirely too short and his bald head was tapered like a lemon. Craziness was in his movements and eyes. Behind him in the foyer an oval Victorian mirror displayed his back, and below the mirror on an antique bureau covered in white silk tulle were the strewn fragments of a broken vase.

"You must be somebody, I suppose." He blinked. "And God almighty, I suppose it's still raining."

"You suppose a lot."

"I suppose I do."

"Dear," the man yelled in mock singsong. "The whore is here." Casually he flung a brown trench coat suavely over his arm. "I am the lady's husband," he said by way of an introduction. "Richard Longtree, nee Halleck."

"You should know."

"You're Jome, is that right?"

"You remind me of a publicist," I said.

The little man grinned as though I'd given him a compliment.

"I'm not a publicist. But I do have a couple of them. I'm actually just leaving."

"I like the way that sounds when you say it."

"I hope you enjoy the concert," Richard said. "I'll be there myself."

Switching the coat to his other arm, he said, "I know what you're after, Jome. Papery little green things and a way to get more out of my wife. But your great sin is how typical you are."

I took hold of the lapels of Richard's polo shirt.

"This is exactly what I mean," he said. "This kind of violence. Typical."

Later I'd regret—a little—bashing him in the nose, but at the time there seemed no better alternative. Sue's husband was thrown back into the bureau, a chaos of khaki and churlishness. Transparent slices of the mirror skittered around him, getting snatched in his hair. Even before he landed he was already dusting himself off.

Sue's heels echoed across the tiled floor. She hovered over

the mess, peering from me to her spouse, and finally stayed on me.

"If I had a penny for every time Richard was bounced in the foyer I'd have almost a nickel," she said.

"I'm not sure why I did that," I said.

The dress she had on was dark and glittery. In the precise light of the place it matched her eyes, and seemed to have been molded onto her body by a master ceramicist. Silver earrings with diamond inlays dangled just above her shoulder blades, and she held her green clutch like it was going to scamper off. Her red hair was slicked to the side.

Then I remembered that there was a guy on the floor.

"I'm really glad you did that," Richard Longtree said, shaking glass off himself. "I'm really very glad." He started toward the door, leered at Sue and then at me, and walked solidly out. Climbing into his diminutive car he shouted, "I am glad he did that. Proves my point." The Peugeot's engine blared and Richard Longtree yelled something as he drove off.

"What's his problem?" I asked.

The yellow specks in her eyes glowed like goldmines from a thousand feet up. "Me," she said.

Her car was the green Jaguar, one hue off from her dress and two from her eyes. It was a four-seater affair and the leather upholstery was like reclining on the sounds a clarinet makes when it's blown well. She squealed out of the driveway and made a few sharp turns. Less than a quarter of a mile brought us to the baronial, Deco-trimmed cultural center that appeared to have been borrowed from Rome and took up one entire city block on 5th Street.

Our seats in the symphony hall were three rows from the podium. Rich people puttered around in tuxedos and long gowns, doing what they could to appear smug and secure. Beside me an old guy with his mouth open was fanning himself with a single leather glove. I stared at the round ceiling emblazoned with Renaissance art, almost missing Richard Longtree sitting in a private box overlooking us and muttering.

I nudged Sue.

"Your husband is up there in the wings glaring at you."

She just shook her head.

"He does that. And he hates classical music, so you can imagine how much more he hates me if he'd come here."

"What's he trying to accomplish?"

"He's trying to be more like himself every day," she said as the lights dimmed.

A sprightly quartet bounced into the stage lights and bowed, followed by a deep silence of coughs and sighs. Someone a few rows back was talking in a loud tone. The first violinist turned and stared severely at the person until somebody near him must have pointed out that he was being obnoxious.

"I hate people," Sue whispered.

The low, hungry growls of Schubert's 15th String Quartet grunted out into the soaring acoustics, the slow and frantic opening bars leading abruptly into a sweet lament, which turned, impulsively, into the unhinged outbursts that drew me to Schubert. His music was the stillness and the wildness of pure insomnia. Schubert had always done something to me, all that rambunctious wandering and sociopathic fixation on the elusive theme. Like walking along a path alone, where the moon is everywhere, and the path is dangerous and infinite. It's the innocence of sleep, interrupted by the most agitated dreams. The feeling was one I knew well.

Playing the slow, throbbing second movement, the musicians struggled, tippling from side to side like they'd just alighted from a cruise ship and didn't know how to act on land.

"You like this stuff, don't you?" Sue whispered.

"Of all the things I don't like it would be an example of something I can stand, sure."

"What about it do you like?" Sue's face was inquisitive, but even then it did not lose its derisive smirk.

"I like how anybody can make anything they want out of what they hear," I said.

"Is that it?"

"No, but I couldn't be articulate enough to explain and you're not eager enough to understand."

"That might hurt my feelings," she said, aiming her attention back at the stage and the quartet, who were tuning in preparation of the final movement.

"You don't have any feelings," I said. "I've been searching for them since I met you."

"Maybe you've been searching in the wrong places."

I shut up and listened, yet now I wasn't hearing the music

as exclusively. I glanced at Sue. She was absorbed or was trying to be absorbed. She had a way of shifting a guy's atten-
tiveness away from whatever was holding his interest.

Sue clasped my arm throughout the 20 or so minutes of
the quartet performance, tightening her grip at dramatic
moments. I sniffed at her hair—citrus, mint, honey. When the
music ground to a stop she was motionless, her hand trembling against my leg. I assumed that perhaps Schubert had
affected this un-affectable woman as he did me. Schubert
made every thought I'd ever had or action I'd ever taken trivial, meaningless or both simultaneously.

But Sue leaned in very close to my ear and said, "I'm
thirsty."

I stared at her. "That all?" I asked.

"Is there supposed to be something else?"

She'd let go of me and was putting lipstick on.

Richard was leering down comedically, even leveling a
pair of flashing binoculars at us.

"Anyway," Sue said as the orchestra prepared for the next
piece. "They're doing something modern next. Ligeti. Do you
know him? I don't know him. And I don't like the way the
modern stuff makes me feel."

We slipped out during the opening notes. I didn't check to
see if Richard was behind us, but I was sure he was.

"Does he usually do that kind of thing?" I asked.

"Who, Richard? Yes," she said. "For someone who can't
be passionate he certainly has a way of pretending to be
infatuated."

We were outside and Sue had her arm entwined with
mine.

"When's the divorce?" I asked.

"Oh, any day now," she said, and we ran the rest of the
distance to her car and sat a minute in silence while the
wipers labored.

"Where are we headed?" she asked.

Straight out the parking lot we were going 65 miles per
hour. The faster she accelerated the more relaxed her muscles
became. In silhouette her features were grim and implacable,
set hard into that masculine line I'd recognized on first meeting her—focused on something, it seemed, just beyond the
city and just beyond anywhere else.

"I don't care," I said.

"How about Maury's?" she asked.

"Never been."

"Too cosmopolitan?" and she did that smirk.

"Amusing, isn't it? How drab I am."

Her eyes flashed something nasty at me. "I'm nothing special, Harry," she said. "I might look like I am, but what does that signify?"

"It's Harry now."

"It's whatever you want it to be. I don't think you like me very much, although earlier I thought you liked me quite a lot. Why're you being so nuanced?"

"I don't like anyone, and why would you say that?"

"Well, maybe for a few minutes we can be friends."

She drove the car through an alleyway that cut between 7th and 9th Streets. Disgruntled faces flitted by, screaming out epithets I couldn't hear, men and women loitering behind their desperation. On 4th Street Sue gripped the wheel tight and spun into a vacant space.

Outside, Maury's was faintly lit with paper-covered bulbs and little illuminated ponds, where bleak fish cavorted insipidly with artificial seaweed and tiny plastic divers that swayed and looked like they were actually diving. Customers squirmed through the bronze doors in twos and threes, and once they were in the gaudy mauve interior they bunched together in confused groups and demanded tables.

The silver-haired maitre d'hotel took Sue's arm and noted her reservation in a gold-embossed registry. He took both of our arms and led us to the rear of the loud, golden dining room. We were relieved of our coats and informed that the waiter would be along shortly. Then we were shown to a corner niche that resembled a massage parlor, with a pink chiffon drape furnishing us with a mask of privacy. It reminded me of a pun but I couldn't think of the set-up.

"You come here often?" I asked.

"Often enough," she said.

When the waiter arrived and pulled the curtain aside, Sue ordered pale beer, a bottle of 30-year-old Scotch and snifters. I was fine with soda water. The waiter kept arching his eyebrows and it was starting to bother me. As he was pulling the curtain back, I saw a man dressed all in denim gesturing madly at the maitre d'hotel and getting nowhere. He kept pointing at our table, the half-closed palm of his hand displaying some kind of currency.

What do you want?" I asked her when the waiter had departed.

Sue rested her chin on a jeweled fist.

"We're just celebrating how well the case is going."

"Is it going well?" I asked. I played with the napkin ring.

"It is if we're here celebrating it. Also, I don't drink alone. Come along and have one with me."

"No."

"Why not?"

"Because I won't stop till all the fireworks are over."

"I like fireworks."

"I wasn't talking about fireworks."

I put the napkin ring down and looked at Sue's low neckline, the motion of her small muscles and her long, upright neck.

Eyebrows returned with our drinks on a silver tray, alongside two waters. Sue ordered salmon in a honey mustard dill sauce for the both of us, a couple of salads, chilled lemon and dill soup.

"It probably would have been cheaper to buy a fisherman," I said. I parted the curtain. The guy in denim was sitting miserably on a divan in the lounge.

"Tell me who Harry Jome is," she said, handling the beer.

"Sure, but first tell me who the guy in the jean suit is."

Sue dribbled beer on her chin. "I don't know him," she said.

"You didn't even look."

"I don't know anyone who wears jeans. Now drink your Scotch like a good boy."

I touched the snifter, then released it, and while we ate I kept touching, releasing.

"Go ahead," she said. "I won't tell anybody."

"I haven't had a drink in a while," I said. "I don't remember how to do it. I want to drink bad. But I know how bad I am when I drink. And so the answer is, not right now."

I knew I was going to drink, and I could have chosen a moment to do it, but her game was inflating her interest, and so I waited until I couldn't wait.

She smiled at me and then she winked and I capitulated hard and fast, and the liquor was redemption on the back of my throat, washing me with warmth, the earlier pricks of fatigue draining away.

"I forgot how much I like booze," I said. The feeling in my body was the equivalent of wearing a glorious wool shirt.

"I'm sorry," Sue said. "For making you do that."

"No, you're not." I was so soothed by the liquor that I didn't need to have Sue there at all, however nice it was. I felt a small amount like myself, whoever that was, like being an extra in the movie of your life, and so having none of the pressures or awareness of the main character.

I poured my glass to the rim.

Sue was studying me like an experiment at the zoo. Around us the restaurant wasn't so fast-paced. When I pulled the curtain aside, clarity was smeared all over. The meeting of businessmen at the next table, swearing confidentially under their breaths, undoubtedly on the verge of some bank-ruptcy or other. A family eating in silence across the room— the wife not even glancing at the husband or at the kid in the high-chair, a family that soon wouldn't be a family. Waiters scampering with trays and beakers too busy to have any emotions of their own.

"You look nice with a glass in your hand," she said.

Sue was missing that ridiculing expression I knew so well, relaxed now into a curiously erotic gleam I hadn't noticed before the drink.

"So do you, with a glass in my hand," I said.

She reached out her glass and gently clinked mine.

"What shall we drink to?" I asked.

"Nothing," she said earnestly. "Sobriety."

"To nothing and sobriety then." I couldn't stop drinking and I couldn't stop talking. After a while I didn't know what I was saying or drinking. Just that it was right. When the wait-er came back Sue ordered a second bottle of Scotch, and so did I.

The last time I parted the curtain the guy in denim had his head back, asleep.

Two and a half hours later, five or ten glasses of Scotch in my gut and head, I'd babbled everything I knew to Sue Longtree and I didn't even know what I had said or didn't say. She paid a tab that amounted to the gross domestic prod-uct of a small South American capital.

I stopped when we were climbing out of the seat, peering at a table near the exit, where Carol Bergen was peering starkly back over the flame of a candle. She was alone. She saw Sue immediately and started to get up, but gravitated back into her seat.

Carol was as drunk as we were. The collar of her black button-up was wrenched underneath the collar of her gray sweater. The two women stared at each other horrendously as Sue and I approached. Some of my drunkenness fell away just watching the hate stirring between them. Then Sue put a hand out and straightened Carol's collar. Carol slapped her hand away, but Sue showed no indication that her hand had been slapped away and walked, grinning and sauntering, past the maitre d'hotel, who for some odd reason did not look in the least surprised.

"Sorry," I slurred at Carol. "She's having it rough."

"Take your sorry ass and that woman somewhere else," she said, her voice so loud in its hiss that the candle's flame was doused. I tried talking to Carol for a minute, my phrases inarticulate and probably mixed up. Carol didn't look up. "I don't know what you think she is," Carol said. "But whatever it is I hope it's at least half of what she really is. Because if it's that much, you'll smarten and find another someone."

I waited for her to go on, but Carol Bergen simply ignored me.

And then Sue and I were on the sidewalk, arm in arm, and I was swaying wildly in the warm rain, trying to find the car parked seven feet away.

Sue dialed through radio stations as she drove fast with one finger on the wheel. After a few minutes she switched on the headlights and chuckled at the humor in this. It didn't bother me. I was in a terrific stupor. I tried rolling the window down, but locating the knob was too bewildering an act. So I gave up and starting mumbling.

The radio was playing Body and Soul, and the singer's husky, haunted voice slyly hinted that perhaps there was a bottle of rye stowed somewhere that could make all despair seem like a summer jubilee. I believed her.

I was getting drunker and the yellow line weaving in the road was flying toward me as we drove the sordid streets, throttling uptown. Through the rain and the fog rising from the pavement, figures could be seen. Everybody looks the same in a downpour. I was concentrating on the road, how it veered when you least expected it to. My head lolled side to side, like a marionette's in the wind.

"You're a fun drunk, Harry."

Sue sped up, plowing through the pockets of fog and periodically sideswiping a pile of trash bags. Few cars were on the road; those out flashed their lights and sat on the horns. She was jerking the wheel back and forth, once onto someone's lawn, where a sprinkler washed the windshield as we passed. My brain was sloshing around in my head like a tiny man in a large rain slicker and every pothole felt like an invitation to explode.

I muttered something at her. I was so plastered the idea of forming sentences was the same as forming a republic.

"What?" she said.

"I said, you should see the other guy."

"Nice night for a drive, though," she said.

Then I said something indiscernible.

"You're so sad, Harry. What're you so sad about?"

I tried explaining and realized I wasn't saying anything.

Ahead of us a patrol car coincidentally spun around and turned onto a side street. Hands that had once belonged to me clumsily wiped moisture off my face.

"Where the hell is this?" I asked.

"You're still a fun drunk, Harry," she said, tickling my forearm with her fingertips. Had hair not been growing out of my gums I would have leaned over and undressed her thoroughly and quickly and got down to business. As it was I could barely talk.

The slanted lights of a small car had been in the mirror since we'd left the restaurant, and I kept checking. Soon, however, I couldn't even manage that.

For a second I thought I was going to be OK. Then I wasn't OK. When I closed my eyes I saw a buzzing, monochrome structure tailing me in a shade of red that can only be called frantic. I snapped my eyes open. Sue was peering at me and ever so negligently eyeing the night ahead of us.

"That the goddamn rubber factory outside of town?" I asked.

"Who knows?"

We were passing the old factory, and beyond the factory there was only the sheets of rain filling in for the sky. Except for the tail behind us there were no other vehicles.

"I'm stuck, Harry," she said.

"How long have we been driving?"

"But really stuck. That's why I got you. You like mystery stories, don't you?" Sue jabbed a cigarette into her mouth and offered me one. I declined, but she was looking at the road and so I had to push her hand away.

"Is this a mystery story?" I asked.

"Honestly I don't know what kind of story it is. I wish it was a love story."

"I read about love in a dime-store romance once."

"Then you know all about it."

The darkness was far away and too close. Pinging on the roof of the car, the rain sounded like gunfire. There was a smell and it was licorice. We passed a large dog with his paws on a guardrail and a field of refuse where corn had once been. There was a deep gulf right behind my eyelids and a nausea that roamed freely over my body and acrid cigarette smoke and the girl smoking beside me, the one who needed a friend to lick the bitterness off her mouth.

We were just outside of town, and when the city limit sign appeared Sue cut a U-turn on a dirt road lugging off into the hills, and we drove back toward the unsettling lights of the city, a blinking cosmos of heat and waste. For a while we were both so quiet I fell into a half-sleep.

"Harry, what are you thinking about?" she asked.

"Nothing much. The road. The hills. The rain. Wondering what this has to do with your brother."

"Why? You don't like me?"

"I'm not so sure if I do, if we're being honest."

"We're not being honest."

"In that case I do like you."

"You're very ambivalent," she said.

"A lot of people have told me that."

"A lot of people are right."

"Maybe," I said. "But maybe everybody's wrong about everything. And then where are we?"

"We're right here." Sue smiled and then the smile fell off her mouth like it had been borrowed. "You're just sad," she said. "You need to be less sad."

"When was the last time it wasn't raining?" I asked.

Sue turned to me as we went around a bend, and we were suddenly back in the city.

"I don't know," she said with an awful gravity in her

voice.

"I don't either," I said.

Puddles glistened in the street, and all the shops were closed. Still, the city was lit up like it was a magnificent and sunny morning. Houses started to hurry by and I could sense myself vaguely hating, though I couldn't pinpoint what exactly. I watched the rain flitting down the windows like it would not pause, enervated by a thought I could not place on the very tip of my mind.

"I can't find it, Harry," Sue suddenly whispered desperately. "I can't find it and I don't know what I'm looking for because it's gone and I've never had it." Her forehead was on the steering column, hands still clutching the wheel. Maybe she was crying. Maybe after a while all that's left is tears and you drain out and wash away from yourself. Maybe I didn't care about her tears because I had my own. And maybe I cared more than I would have liked to care. The car swerved, and she picked up her head.

"I can't find it anywhere," she said, yanking at her dress and neck. "Goddamnit, Harry. Where is it?"

"What?" I blurted.

"I don't know what."

And then she broke apart and started taking off her clothes while she was still driving. The car bounced onto a curb beside an abandoned, fenced-off lot. Some tall lights shone on an unpainted carousel in the middle of the lot. The grounds were where they plunked the circus when it came to town.

"Dominic Early wouldn't have written it this good," she scoffed through her sobbing.

She needlessly pumped the brake and removed the rest of her clothing, except for her heels and stockings, and piled herself on top of me. Her sweat smelled fresh and luxurious, if sweat can smell that way. After a moment of groping and kissing and tearing at one another, she stopped. I was eating the iodized water of her tears.

"I just want to tease you," she said. "I'm not good enough to do what I want to do and what I want to do is die. You ever feel that way?" She climbed back into the driver's seat and nodded at my lusting face.

"Is this what this is?" I asked her.

"More or less," she said. "No matter what, you're a good

man."

"I don't feel like a good man."

"The best ones never do." Wrenching the door back she got halfway out into the rain and turned back to me.

"Harry, I'm sorry but I can't be here with you right now. I just can't right now."

She loosed the car door and fell onto the sidewalk. In my haze I only gurgled. The door slammed shut and the radio was just a mess of sound. I sat and obtusely regarded the headlights and the enticed mosquitoes shifting in and out of the rain and the digits of the dashboard clock. A car parked alongside and a man's shape was scrutinizing me, his chin barely appearing above the bottom of the window. Whether or not he was a delusion, he was nonetheless wearing a blue sweater. Then the car sped off.

Partly craning around I looked for Sue. Her clothes were sprawled on the front seat where she'd slipped them off, one sleeve partly hanging out the open door. She was nowhere on the street. Not even the street was there, with all the buckets of rain that were coming strong. The warmth of the car was like an embrace and I couldn't imagine disentangling myself from it. I started smiling at Sue, but with a woman like that a smile isn't something that stays around.

Clumsily I thumbed at the radio but it wasn't working and I noticed that it wasn't because the volume was down and I was in no condition to turn it up. Listening to the rain I languished there on the comfortable seat, drifting into intermittent sleep.

It was a quarter to two in the morning.

Four-thirty…

And finally dawn.

The engine was off, and when I tried to turn it over there was only a click like you might hear in your jaw. It was 6:30 when I poured myself out of the car. Pressed under the wipers, two unassertive parking tickets flapped. Sue was gone and the headache throttling my temples caused the rain-slick street to spin.

It had been my first drinks in 20 years, and now it was another scarcely tenable day.

I left the car where it was and walked around a minute on the sidewalk to regain my legs. Then I crumpled down near a hydrant and deposited last night's overpriced dinner and the drinks along with the meal. I disliked Sue for making me dislike myself so much. She'd abandoned me and I couldn't make out why. I was on 15th Street, a couple of buildings up from the bus station. As far as I knew it was Monday or Tuesday. Rubbing my face I was straightaway enraged.

A child with an umbrella approached. Closer, I saw that the child was Leo. He sheltered me under the umbrella.

"Where you been?" he asked.

"Around about."

"Smells like you've been drinking."

"Let it alone."

"Let's chat."

I moved away from him. "I can't deal with you right now," I said.

"I'm not bothering you."

"I appreciate that."

Halfway up the next block, I turned, walking backward.

"Oh, Jome," he shouted. "See you up north. Bring warm clothes, OK?" And he headed in the opposite direction.

I loped down to the corner of 8th and 9th. Probably I should have checked that Sue had returned safely to her house, but instead I compelled myself to my office in an ugly shuffle. The air outside was ruined by stifling garbage, and the burning vomit in my nostrils stank of cumin and asparagus. I was a sick, troubled hubris not good enough to drop dead on a crapshoot's veranda. Even my metaphors were deteriorating.

When I arrived at the Santos Building, I was wearing a coat of rain on my back.

Outside my office, I could hear two pairs of hands rummaging through files and drawers. I peeled the door back to find Parker and Porter bent in fat, dumb postures of searching. They didn't notice me right away. Both were in bright seersucker outfits with not enough starch in the collars, their hats aligned on my desk. They were passing around a cigarette as they labored.

"Where is it?" Porter said.

"It's somewheres in here."

Parker twisted his big head and saw me glaring at him.

"He's right here," Parker said to Porter, snapping his fingers.

Porter's jowls were glistening and he puffed the cigarette, handed it to his partner, and breathed out smoke with a question. "Where is it?" he asked me.

"It's somewheres in here," Parker said, giving the cigarette back.

Watching them fumble sent a nostalgic twinge through my body over the death of vaudeville. I said, "So what's the comedy?"

"Ain't no comedy, Jome," Porter said.

Parker: "More along the lines of a fucking drama."

"Uh huh," Porter said.

"Hi, Harry," Parker said. He pointed to Porter with a giant thumb. "Porter, you remember Harry Jome."

"Oh yeah," Porter said. "You were saying he's nothing much."

"Good to see you fellows," I said. I took off my coat and draped it on the back of the chair. I was absent my pistol and there was nothing to be done save try to reason with these funny baboons. But I wasn't in the mood to reason with anyone. My head was splitting. All I wanted was to lie on the floor and groan. "Look, I'm not in such a good mood. Stop by a little later and show me your repartee then."

"We were just making sure," Parker said. "That we hadn't missed anything."

"And what is your hypothesis?" I was edging toward the

filing cabinets.

"That we hadn't missed anything," Porter said.

Parker and Porter were standing close together, their wide bodies nearly wall-to-wall. Porter's suit was missing every single button, and he'd tried to offset this by keeping the flaps of his suit-coat back with his elbows.

"It's getting more cloudy," Porter said, glancing out the window. "And I'm going to get dark in a minute."

I laughed and Parker laughed too. "So what am I fucking laughing at and what am I fucking looking for?" Parker asked.

I shrugged. "Could be anything."

"OK," Porter said. "So what do you think we're looking for, because we are looking for something or else we wouldn't be here, would we." The light caught his face and there was a furrowed dimple in the center of his chin. He went on, "Fact is I don't want to get any darker than I have to."

"Or the situation, too," Parker added.

"What is the situation?" I asked.

In tandem they were coming out from either side of the desk like two lunatics recently signed out. Parker reached into his waistband and dug something out. His big hand looked as though it were eating the gun it held. "See?" he said. "Now I have a gun. And this gun is your fucking gun. It was in the drawer."

"I know," I said.

"Whatever the situation is, a gun changes it," Porter said.

"You still haven't told me what the situation is? What're you looking for?" I asked.

Porter rested his ass on the desk, tilting it forward. Then he straightened up as though his mother had told him not ever to sit on furniture.

"The situation," Parker said, scratching his neck with the barrel of the gun, "is what you're going to tell us it is."

"You working for Sue Longtree?" I asked.

"Why would we be working for her?" Porter said. I stared at his dimple until it formed into a second dimple, and this one winked at me.

"That's my next question."

Parker came in close to me and jabbed me on the shoulder with the metal. I grabbed at the spot and swayed.

"I wish you wouldn't do that," I said. "I was out drinking

last night and I'm feeling pretty lousy today."

"I thought you liked problems," Porter said, staring at Parker.

"Not when they look like you."

"Open the window," Parker said. "It's getting fucking complex in here."

Porter heaved the window up. Dainty clods of rain tiptoed onto the sill. Porter stayed by the window to dry his sweat and blink in the wind. "This is no Ritz-Carlton," he said.

"What's so great about the Ritz-Carlton?" I asked.

"You ever stayed at one?"

"No."

"We just need some air for thinking," Parker said. "You going to tell us what we're looking for?"

"Hopefully a couple new suits," I said. Parker slammed me in the shoulder again and the pain swelled. Compared to the hangover, it was almost an intercession.

"It don't look so fucking good, does it?" he asked.

"No," his partner said. "It doesn't look good for someone in particular."

Parker took a few steps back and forth and planted himself once again in front of me.

"You're doing something with the female Longtree." He raised the gun to his cheek and scratched a red, splotchy razor-burn. "Our client is inquisitive about that."

A stealthy breeze took some of my papers out the window and shuffled more that were on the desk.

"Maybe," I said. "Would you mind shutting the window? I'd like to keep my office in here."

The two men glanced at one another, not knowing how to proceed. Tension was so heavy you could have cut it with a tablecloth.

"Maybe," Porter said. "But probably definitely."

"Why have you scoped out Ben Bergen?" Parker asked.

"He killed himself in a motel room upstate."

"What he's asking is why you're looking at it, if I'm not mistaken," Porter said. He came away from the window and moisture was running down his face.

"Because he killed himself in a motel room upstate."

Parker itched his face again with the muzzle. His partner picked up the Dominic Early novel and flipped it over. "Hey, one of these things," he said.

One swift thrust and my toe caught Parker in the shin. His left foot rolled over on the marble I'd dropped a few days before and he flailed like a goon, clutching at the air. The gun startled his finger and the blast took away a part of the right side of his head. His gaze stayed intact and dumb. Porter grappled with slippery hands past the desk, tripped over his partner's toe and lunged for the open door.

"Wait a minute," Parker said crisply, stunned and numb and dying. He toppled over backward and landed with an explosive thud similar to the gun's yell. I could hear Porter frantically descending the staircase, followed by a pitiful yelp and a crash below. And then there was just the breathless calm of a man deciding what the hell he should do. Choral murmurs wafted throughout the building.

I poked through Parker's second-hand wardrobe, extracted his billfold to find the miscellany of a pretty stultifying guy in a struggle with mid-life. Creased dollar bills. Photos of nieces and nephews. A playing card with a nude woman and the phrase "Everybody Ends Up in St. Louis" on it. In one pocket there was a penknife and a tiny flashlight, and the other held a scrap of expensive stationary with the words *Find It*. Throughout the excavation I did my best not to look at what was left of Parker's face. The room was splattered with what I didn't want to notice.

Digging into his breast pocket I unearthed a cheap memo book, clamped with a rubber band. The first entry in his adolescent shorthand was just a name and an address: Richard Longtree, Melancthon Hotel, 1st Street, Room 304.

Underneath that: Evidence for Divorce Proceedings Detailing the Extra-Marital Affairs of Susan Longtree.

A few pages later I came to a transcription of my wayward discussion with Sue at the diner.

I flipped to the last bunch of text: *Going to confront HJ for information. Richard is getting impatient with the case. Will terminate contract if nothing in three days.* I ripped all the pages out of the notebook that referenced me and littered the remnants out the window. I left the long passages containing laundry lists and grocery reminders. Stuffing the data back into his pocket my finger fell through the hole of a wedding ring. I shook it off. Stains from underneath Parker spread in all directions, like a flower or like what it was. I should have called somebody, but since I'd never had a dead guy in my office before, I wasn't too sure what the protocol was supposed to be. I did know, however, that if I was almost sure not to have gotten any sleep before, it was a granite certainty that I would not be sleeping now.

A jumbled scent of disgusting sweetness filled the room.

I didn't know what to do so I didn't do anything but stare at the blood and at Parker's buffoonish suit and his dying, open-eyed squint and his blood on the wallpaper. Rain was soaking my back and I let it. Even indoors I couldn't get away from the rain.

This was all Sue Longtree.

It was times like these I wished I'd taken up ballroom dancing and stuck to it.

A half hour later the detective, a crooked trilby set squarely on his sloping forehead, came in with two lock-stepped uniforms stuffed with young brutal men. The detective's eyes and movements were shy or calculating, and a fine buzz cut gave his gray hair a spectral quality when he removed the hat, as though he were going to mutate into a black and white image of himself at any second. I gauged him at about 50 or a little older. Hand tailored, his gray suit was tight-fitting and he had a green stem in the breast pocket without a flower attached. A gray mustache was on his lip, one tapered end longer than the other.

His officers prodded Parker until he told them to go stand outside the door. With a little pencil he lifted Parker's hand, bent and sniffed at the gun and struggled to slip it into his pocket with the pencil.

"That's my property," I said. The detective didn't acknowledge me as he poked around the room.

"Did you touch anything?" he asked, and his words came out in a monotonous stream. The kind of voice you'd hear broadcasting financial updates.

I was exhausted and hungover. Now would be an unparalleled time to say something stupid and I did my best. "Just my hands."

"Jome, I'm Leslie Cowper—lieutenant right now—and I hate my job, so if you make it difficult for me I'm going to make me difficult for you. Go ahead and sit down."

"I'm already sitting."

"Why don't you close that window?" Cowper said.

I got up and closed the window and returned to my chair.

For a while longer Cowper prodded Parker's head.

"You got a chair?" he asked.

"No. There's only one and you told me to sit down and I'm sitting down."

Cowper thrust his face into the hallway and called for one of the officers to bring in a chair and one of the officers brought in a chair. He put his hat back on when he eased himself into the seat across from me, reposed like he didn't care. White socks were revealed as he crossed his legs. His round jawline pumped up and down.

"So," he said. "So explain this to me."

He put the pencil behind his right ear and didn't have a notepad.

"Well," I started, and the throbbing in my head began, not quite as insistently. "The guy on the floor is Parker—not sure about the first name, could be Parker, but you're a cop for some reason—and this Parker guy was scratching the side of his head with the gun when the gun went off and that's the cause of his malaise."

"Guy doesn't usually itch himself with a bullet."

"You didn't know this guy."

"What was he doing here?" Cowper asked. He removed the pencil and let it frolic across his knuckles, keeping his eyes on it.

"Just itching," I said.

"Was that your gun in his hand?"

"I think so, judging by the initials."

"Who the hell keeps their initials on a gun? Are you a child or something?"

"I was kidding."

"Don't." Cowper strained forward. "Any decent idea how your gun ended up in his hand and your bullet in his head?"

"I imagine he picked it up. And while I'm on the topic, is someone going to clear him away or should I invest in an air freshener and expect that he'll help out with the rent, because—"

"When did you get here?"

"About 20 minutes ago."

"This guy was already here?"

"Yeah, him and this other guy."

"This other guy?"

"Porter."

Cowper steadied his gaze into mine. His pencil fell and he stooped to pick it up with immense irritation.

"I think you're being difficult," he said.

"I wouldn't."

"What you've said doesn't sound like a good defense at all."

"Am I defending myself?"

"I don't know. I just got here." Suddenly he pointed the eraser tip at me. "If I were you," he said. "I'd hire somebody better equipped to handle your legal business, and, oh yeah, what is your business?"

"This and that."

"You don't have to be so specific. Private dick, I guess. You got a license, Jome? From the county? To practice what you're doing?"

"I'm not practicing. I'm actually doing it."

"No license, huh?" Cowper grimaced emphatically. "That's too bad. You got to have one or things like what happened happen."

"I have a driver's license," I said.

"Don't use it until this is all cleared up, and if you do use it, use it real well."

I put my hands behind my head. Cowper had a hardness in his brown, doughy eyes that was just a little terrifying. He pulled a bent cigarette from behind the ear without the pencil and stuck it in his mouth without lighting it.

"I believe you, Jome," he said, the cigarette tottering. "Don't ask me why."

"OK. Why?"

"Because I said so. I don't like anything self-apparent, because what looks that way typically isn't."

He tried blanking out a tar stain on his fingernail with the worn eraser. He got bored and studied the blood-patterned carpet, then trained his attention on the corpse.

"What do you think?" he asked Parker. As Cowper stood he tossed the pencil into the wastepaper basket in the corner. "This have something to do with a case?" he asked, taking the pathetic cigarette and sticking it in back of his ear again.

"I couldn't really say."

"Something about a Longtree?"

I flung my hands up.

"If I knew anything," I said. "I wouldn't be doing this."

"Ever hear the name Dean Bruckner?" he asked.

"Not even once."

"Since I can't tell when you're lying or not, I'll just be an idealist and assume you never are. Bruckner called this minor massacre in from a payphone next door. He wouldn't say what he was doing hanging around here, but he's a private dick like you. Are you working with him?"

"I don't know this fellow but I'm sure he's good."

Cowper nodded, and kept nodding. "He is good. Better than you, I bet." His sweet, boyish face was sweating and placid, like somebody who's just found out what sex is for.

Cowper was at the door, his soles making squishing sounds.

"Oh," he said over his shoulder. "There's another dead fellow down in the front hall. Seems you shouldn't jump down stairs thirty at a time."

"That would be Porter," I said. "Ran out when his partner re-decorated my walls."

"Why do you suppose he jumped down all those stairs?"

"Maybe he was in a hurry."

Cowper got up, tugged the brim of his trilby. "See you again soon," he said. Leaving, he took hold of the chair and brought it out with him. His outline was in the glass door as he motioned to someone and then it wasn't and the elevator was groaning with too many bitter men.

I was doing nothing but thinking of Sue Longtree and her pretentious shit, Richard, the crumb who'd hired the guys I'd now done away with. It was all too bad. Not to mention the rain and the body on the floor, who'd fulfilled nothing more insidious than a mindless routine divorce job.

"If only you understood," I said to Parker, " how much of this I don't understand."

The meat grinder drove up outside and two burly asocial types stamped into my office bearing a gurney between them. One of the kids was wearing a sailor hat, tattoos running up and down his arms. They zipped up the fat man and heaved him on the gurney; the outlines of the former Parker bulged as his remains were hurried away. The boys lingered a moment foreseeing a tip, and I ignored them conclusively.

My loneliness was harsh. Nothing looked especially promising except that the two dicks were off my back, which was a relief. But now I had to contend with the Longtrees.

Sue didn't answer when I called. I was rather dizzy. This would have been a perfect moment to contact my attorney, if I had one. Maybe even a prostitute or an acupuncturist. Some kind of small dog to keep me company.

The stain on the carpet wasn't going anywhere. I reached the elevator starving, afraid that food would disrupt me completely. My stomach fell sharply as the elevator clanked down. Watching the floor ascend I was reminded of the two private eyes who wouldn't be molesting elevators anymore.

My two options for the day were to either whine about it or buy some mineral water at the store around the corner.

The first evidence I could see of the person on the ground floor was his tennis shoes. Then corduroy pants and a blue sweater. At last his face was there, a gray goatee and matching short hair.

"Jome?" he asked before I could pry apart the grate.

"Some other time," I said.

"I'm on a job for somebody and I need to talk to you about somebody." He spoke fast and his sweater sleeves were too short and rode the tops of the wristwatches he had on both wrists.

"Who's that?"

"A guy by the name of Wald. My client is interested in him about something important. And maybe about you too, as you've become rather important as well. OK? So where does that stand us? Wald has been on me and I'm a little less than positive it has something to do with you."

"Who's your client?"

"You know I can't tell you that, but I know you know what I'm talking about."

"You know a lot."

"I know what I need to know. I know I need to have this wrapped up fast. In case you're wondering, my name is Sid Lewishom."

"I wasn't wondering."

"My name is still Sid Lewishom."

"And I still wasn't wondering." I started past him, but he kept sidestepping in the way. "I'm busy," I said.

"I am too. It's a private matter. And this other guy has been stuck on me and I don't like it and I thought maybe—"

"Yeah," I interrupted. "You thought maybe."

"I thought maybe it might have to do with a few other

people."

"I don't know anything about a few other people."

"No one does. It could benefit the both of us is what I see."

"Now you're being interesting. But you're still not being too interesting."

"I'll buy you a drink and you'll see how interesting I can be."

"Another night you can buy me a drink. I'm not in the mood to see how interesting anybody is."

"Lookit," he yelled.

"No," I said. He didn't follow me into the street, and when I came out of the store with a bottle of mineral water he wasn't in sight.

I went around to Cramm's. The tailor was sitting on the front stoop of the building that housed his shop, roofed from the rain by his awning. He was leafing through a sewing machine manual when I came up to him and knocked the book onto his shoes.

"Where's the suit?" I snapped.

"I'm working on it," Cramm said. He retrieved the manual and flipped to find his page.

"Right now you are?"

"Well, I'm thinking about working on it," he said.

"It doesn't look like you're working on anything." I kicked Cramm's wingtip with my own. "Cramm," I said, "this has been a bad week for me and that suit would come in handy about now." His sunken eyes took nearly 30 seconds to rise and meet mine. "I'm going to come back in a day or two and that goddamned suit had better be stitched together by then."

Cramm was nonplussed and closed his sewing book. "I have nine pairs of pants that the Elks Club want hand-done for a conference they're having this week. So it's kind of a position to be in."

"You can deal with the Elks Club or you can deal with me." I scoffed and turned away. "I'll be in the area, Cramm. I hope you get the point of me really wanting this suit."

"I get that feeling," Cramm said. "I get that feeling all over me."

I had to see Sue. Bitterness and frustration welled in me, compounded by the rain and building into a nasty rage. Added to that, the mineral water wasn't soothing my stomach at all.

I walked the drenched streets for the remainder of daylight, observing the sky shift from gray to black to a color that was neither. Imagining what I would say to Sue Longtree and how I would quit her and how I wouldn't be able to.

On 3rd Street the branches of indistinguishable trees fluttered in the windswept odium of befouling rain. The headlines of a gusting newspaper bellowed that the trashmen's union hadn't yet reached a compromise on their strike.

I wasn't very curious about this Lewishom fellow but I was about Perle and how he was involved—and why. I assumed that since the guy had only shown up after my visit to Perle, the big insurance man had only brought him in since my visit. But what did Perle and his expensive hair have to do with it? Or Wald? For that matter, Sue Longtree herself, the tentacled nexus from which all else was being somehow jockeyed?

There were too many people in this town, and they were all aimed at me. The cast was bloating, and not a single sympathetic role in the whole lousy production.

I rang the bell at Sue's. The ivied walls looked disconsolate, and the place had the extended quiet of being uninhabited. Twice I rang the bell and watched the wet leaves swirl around my ankles on the dry porch.

A boy rode by on a bicycle, colorful cards in the spokes clipping peacefully, in the act of wiping the water from his eyeglasses.

An airplane cut noiselessly through low clouds, and soon its twin engine was audible in the darkening veil.

I was thinking of the Longtree family, a domestic unit of murder and suicide that would have compared quite well to Leopold and Loeb on any day. Sue Longtree was nothing but the closest representation of how secluded we really are in the defiant madness lying uncontrolled just behind what we think we are or what we want others to think we are.

And more importantly, why was I standing here wasting time when I could have been somewhere else wasting time?

I was feeling worse than my conception of awful.

I turned and was heading down the stairs when a magnified cigarette lighter sputtered in a car window across the narrow street. It was a white Ford two-seater in extreme dilapidation. Behind the fogged driver's side window a man with a long head was looking at me. It wasn't Wald or

Lewishom, but that's as far as I got on his identification before the door behind me clicked.

"Hi," Sue said to my back.

At once I ascended the stairs and slapped her terribly on the cheek, the slap ringing and torching my hand. Sue touched the blushing spot.

"You didn't have to do that," she said, her eyes watering.

"I had to do something, didn't I? It was the first thing that came to mind. I didn't know what else to do."

Partly clothed in a light blue bathrobe and unnecessary heels, Sue's hair was done up in a pink towel, a stray eyelash on her cheek.

"You look like you've been up for weeks designing a submarine," she said.

"Who's the guy in the Ford?" I asked. "Who the hell is Wald? Why's this Lewishom trying to corner me? You know what I've been doing this morning?"

"Come inside and apologize," she said. She led me inside and latched the door behind us. "Why don't you take off your jacket and act like a person for a minute?"

"It's hard for me to do that around you. I asked a second ago if you know what I've been doing this morning."

"You don't seem like you can do much around me," she said. "And I'm not causing any of these problems."

I wanted to slap her again. "How about Dean Bruckner?" I shouted out. "Or Cowper, or Perle? You know the game." I must have resembled a lunatic, because Sue's eyes widened. "Tell me."

"No," she said. "I can't tell you what I can't tell you."

Before I could do the opposite of protest, she was practically inside my mouth, gnawing on my lower lip and drawing the blood out, pressing herself against me like a horny leech. Her body smelled of cocoa butter and lavender shampoo.

I loosened the knot on her robe and used my hands, clumsy on her lower back, spine, hips. It had been a while and I was hungry and I tried having her entire body at once.

"You're so sad," she breathed.

"I'm not sad," I said into her mouth. "How could I be sad?"

Her eyes were misty and unfocused, as though she were in two places at once and couldn't figure out how to reassemble.

The robe sank around her feet and onto my shoes. I was

being dragged up the ornate staircase toward the darkened hallway, an amateur in the business, my hands behaving as though they'd never touched anything soft before. I gently rubbed at the prickly stubble between her legs and we lost our balance and had to grab at the oak balustrade. I shoved my index finger inside her and she twitched, putting one rigid hand onto my pants to unbuckle my belt while the other rubbed at my face brutally, simultaneously pushing me back and drawing me in.

We zigzagged into the hall, leaving extraneous clothes behind, knocking into a table, slamming into an oil painting of a woman sunbathing. A flash of gaping doorways, a bathroom cupboard, a statue on a glass pedestal, a full-length mirror, rummaging into each other's bodies like imbeciles at a bank run.

"Let me make you less sad," she whispered. "You're so sad it hurts."

"All right."

"You're a sad man and I'm a sad woman."

The chenille drapes weren't drawn in the bedroom and the view was of the tops of spruce trees and the sparkling lights of the city's tallest buildings washed in the manic rain. It was a plain room with a four-poster bed, an unlit vanity set with a black typewriter and a page wavering. We stumbled over a footstool, plopped onto a loveseat for a moment, and finally located the contours of the bed.

She was astride me, knees tight around my chest, her face pale, head thrown back like she was faking the laughter that comes after a bad joke told by someone you sort of like.

Somewhere in the house a radio was going softly, an impressionistic piano trio. I unfastened her red bra, but she snapped it back on and I didn't argue.

"Tell me what makes you so sad," she kept whispering.

"Not being here with you."

"Please, tell me. I have to know."

I gasped and then she gasped. When she came she hiccuped and covered her mouth with her hand. Then our bodies were as immobile and unapproachable as curdled milk on an expensive porcelain saucer. She rolled onto her side away from me and pulled the blanket over her head. I had a desire for words, but I did not act on it and kept myself quiet.

There was a circus of Longtrees in my dream, some in

period costume and others current, segued and dark-eyed, ready to slaughter one another at the drop of a glance. They'd congregated in a vast, dead field where indeterminable fruit was being harvested, packed into crates lain waiting in the rears of white trucks, and driven off with a groan of antique engines.

I wandered among them, searching for Sue, wholly lost in the enormous, apparently endless orchard that had borne every single goddamn one of them and looked to be in some kind of golden age.

One youthful Longtree drank vinegar from a clear glass cup.

Another was plucking grass and eating it.

And a third, a woman, watched me longingly from the restive spot under a tree.

I counted the rough patches of cloud overhead. The horizon in every direction—a blisteringly off-white sunset—was as fake as a Hollywood backdrop. Brushstrokes could be seen clearly, and streaks of paint dripped down from the convex sky, forming puddles at the base of this fake world.

For a dreamscape, it was the work of a dilettante craftsperson.

On the other side of the field a figure with stooped shoulders mourned inaudibly. It was Sue. I approached her and saw that she was cutting desperately into the skin of a dull red apple with a razor-blade. Her grin fairly jumped off her face. Then her lips compressed into a dismal frown.

"Does the breeze have a kind voice?" she asked.

She kept slicing through the flesh of the apple but there was nothing inside and soon she was empty-handed, pouting, counting something in the air, and then she was pointing at my throat with a look of horror.

Liquid was spilling across my neck toward the back of my head. I blotted the spot, trying to make it ebb, but the warmth was relentless.

Then something happened.

I woke panicked. The ceiling was drifting away into a recklessly speeding fan that I could not follow. I tried to keep my eyes fixed on a single rotor but lost it in the whirring motion.

Sue Longtree was straddling me again; her eyes were shut tight, mascara and tears staining her cheeks. I felt the razor digging into my neck, gliding effortlessly toward my adam's apple. I was in shock, more from the disturbingly tranquil expression on her face than the fact that she was cutting my throat open. A rush of hot blood streamed around me, wetting the sheets. She was parting me very carefully. I shifted but she wouldn't budge, then I tried pushing her away, but her dead weight was immovable.

I had her wrist and slapped her with my free hand, and then I slapped her harder. Weakness was slopping all over me like a newly bathed animal, subduing me totally. I thrashed and I yelled and stammered. Still she slept and used the razor-blade. Soon I was only gagging and sputtering.

Dying is just the fear of dying. I savored and chewed my breath as though it were poisoned oatmeal.

The final image that would throw me into the Questionable would be a somnambulist woman carving her initials in my neck and the ceiling fan like a cryptic areola above her red hair.

Finally I socked her so densely in the side of the head that my knuckles or her cheekbone cracked, and she toppled off the bed with a flicker of green eyes, giving me another valedictory swipe of the blade as she was pushed off. She landed on the floor with a thud and a little shriek that was uttered in a voice that didn't belong to her.

I rolled onto my stomach, stanching the wound with the pillow. Things once clear in the room were becoming disconcertingly imprecise. The clock was a tiny explosion of numerals, the furniture just billowing wooden figures, the whole room a rotten womb with no logic. Trying to stand I fell into the nightstand, stuttered a few mumbled phrases, and was out well before the hardwood floor caught me.

While I napped in the comfy embrace of dying Sue had tied one of her husband's monogrammed handkerchiefs around my cut neck. The bleeding temporarily slowed but left behind a lacerating pain that killed any urge to speculate very lucidly. Fifty-one percent of that pain was rage. With her unwanted help I staggered into the bathroom, bowed my head into the spotless sink, and washed my face with miserably cold water.

"Go away," I told her when she put a hand on my shoulder. "Not a good time." And she did. In the mirror I watched her getting back into her bathrobe, and her body was arousing for a second, and then it was nothing.

Carefully, I unwrapped the tourniquet so that the clinging fabric didn't jerk my skin off. I soaked the grinning gash with a cupped hand. The agonizing tang of water lasted awhile. I gripped the faucet with my other hand to steady myself. I stood at the sink for five minutes, my mind amok, trembling.

She came into the mirror looking worse than I did, her left cheek a wheel of greenish brown, top lip cracked and bloated. Red strands of hair stuck to the glib sweat on her brow.

"You could have at least used shaving cream," I said. She was crying now and trying skittishly to hold back the tears.

"I'm sorry, Harry," she said, sliding two arms around me. I slipped out of her reach and into the bedroom, scrutinizing her disconsolate reflection from a freakish angle and pretending that I wasn't going to pass out from the pain, from lack of sleep.

"I'm sorry for how you must be feeling right now," I said. Neither of us were dazzled by my clever parlance.

She was all pinched up, scowling like a dog. I hunched forward on a footrest, gathered my shoes on. I tied the laces as though I were focused on some algebraic problem that had been baffling men for centuries.

"I was sleeping when I did it," she breathed. "I couldn't know what I was doing. Now you know why I hired you."

I got my shoes laced and realized that they were the only clothes I'd put on. My ratty suit and trousers were scattered in the sheets and I quickly untangled them and dressed brusquely.

"That's no excuse," I said. "And I only half believe you. I knew you were a bitch. I didn't know why. I still don't know why."

"I can't help it," she said. "I had a dream that I was doing it and I awoke and I was doing it."

"I'm through," I said, zipping my pants. "With you, I mean."

"Keep the money."

"I wasn't considering not keeping the money. But I'm not quitting yet. This scenario is going to be solved whether you like it or not."

"There isn't any solution," she said. "It's gone on long enough."

"What's that mean?" I grabbed her roughly by the arm and shook her. She wrenched free and sat on the bed, head bowed, hands splayed on her knees.

"I don't mean anything," she said. "I've never meant anything."

"What's gone on long enough?" I asked.

"Everything."

"You're not making any sense, Ms. Longtree."

Sue burst into a crying fit that lasted a few seconds. It was strange not to feel remorse or a pang of sympathy for the woman, but I felt neither.

"So now you know about yourself," I said. "You like to murder people in their sleep after sex. Like the rest of the Longtrees, apparently." I paused and gave her my worst frown. Her sobs were coming in short huffs. "So you know. So now what?"

Sue raised her head, searching my face for some kind of reassurance. She found none.

Her crying grew soft but persistent, like she'd been saving a lifetime's worth of stifled reactions for the right moment and just realized it wasn't the right moment but couldn't shove it all back in. With her knees pulled up to her chest on the disheveled bed Sue suddenly looked tiny and far away. Perhaps I should have forgiven her, consoled her, told her truths about how screwed up she was, at bottom a kind woman, possibly, with nowhere to put her kindness. Something, however, about how afraid she looked made me even more merciless.

My brain was clumsy and it took me two minutes to button my shirt.

"I haven't been this sad in a long time," she said.

"I believe you. You're making advances."

She clutched the neckline of her bathrobe together, eyes just a muted, watery green, mouth weak and closed. She hadn't dyed her hair in days, and for the first time I spotted brown roots thrusting at the red.

Sue was sobbing my name.

"Harry, I have to tell you something."

"I don't want you to tell me anything because nothing you say is worth listening to and I've heard it anyway." I knotted my tie, forgetting the condition of my neck, and a searing stab of pain shot to my chin, reinvigorating my indignation.

On a shelf there was a row of colorful books, and on a few of the bindings was the big name of Dominic Early in goofy font.

"Who the hell is this goddamn Early guy?" I shouted at her.

She looked up, and when she did, I couldn't look at her. Without difficulty I opened the door.

"This needs to go different," she said.

"What does?"

"This whole story. I don't like how it's going."

For a second I glanced at her, lost in her own mind, bruised, childish, shaking. The hallway was demure, wider than I recalled, splattered with calm hues of blues and whites, of figurines and round shapes and a tinsel ceiling. I eased the door closed soundlessly.

I waited for her to follow me out so that I could leave her again. Soon the sobbing stopped and another door clicked shut.

There was a drawing of the orchard, this one unframed, stuck to the wall with two strategic pushpins. It was sloped to the left. I felt the need to straighten it. A radio somewhere was playing opera. Cherubini, I thought. I'd never liked Cherubini much, never less so than now.

I hastened out like a nihilist at village choir practice. Torrents of rain pounded the pavement, punched my aching body, the pain radiating down from the smile in my neck as I ambled across the lawn, avoided the spitting sprinkler that sounded as though it were wishing me a loony farewell.

I stumbled through the vacant neighborhoods of the dusky morning, oblivious to the dimwitted paper boy in green hauling a sack of early editions over his shoulder, the delivery trucks, past the overnight factory men pulling dismally into driveways to sleep badly until the next shift, the knocked-down lawn ornaments and the weeping willows, the crows nibbling at overflowing garbage bins. Wives closed mailboxes with pops and sorted through letters and coupons. Bending into someone's garden I plucked a larkspur and studded it into my breast pocket.

The handkerchief was coming undone and I had to continuously keep from handling it as a shot of mad torment devoured me. I knocked into brick walls and telephone poles, wanting to vomit like I had never wanted anything else in my life.

I don't know why in hindsight, but I was making for the Bergen residence. Other than not dying, the money in my freezer was the only claim I had, and Carol Bergen seemed the best person to feel sorry for myself with. I no longer had any idea what I was doing. What's more, a mean notion hit me over and over—I hadn't known what I'd been doing for quite a while.

My aspirations dwindling, the great big clumsy solution struck me. A second later the enlightenment was lost in my creaking thoughts, and I couldn't be sure what I had grasped.

At the Bergen place the little kid, Dot, met me on the porch. She was a fragile, brown-haired child eating apple sauce out of a blue plastic bowl with her hands. Her eyes were deeper and grayer than a child's should have been. I was swaying on the top step. The street was too wet and too glistening and all of a sudden too hot to stand in.

The kid screamed. I patted my throat. The handkerchief was lying on my shoe, the rain rinsing it clean. Dot ran behind the screen door, small and dark against the interior of the house. Carol was shouting for her from the backyard.

"It's OK," I said to the kid. "Jome is OK. Just give him a minute."

While I was stooping for the handkerchief, I toppled onto my head and heard, briefly, five million pairs of heels marching toward me. The sidewalk was moist and agreeable and I could have lain there for days. Hands prodded me, voices yelled, and all I could think of was my tailor's extraordinary incompetence and how upset I was that the suit wasn't finished yet.

I was floating in a vacuum and then I was tumbling back to earth, but maybe I didn't want to be tumbling back to earth. I might have screamed out, or sobbed and spasmed, but I knew it was a delusion and I knew it was fleeting. It was that static elsewhere I recalled from my alcohol-induced fever days, a particular kind of location that doesn't have any geography or depth.

I dreamed of my unfinished suit like it was a religious icon. It clothed a mannequin with my build and no face, glowing in an empty shop that wasn't Cramm's. I reached out to caress the fabric, and that's when the arms of the suit shot out, tossing a bucket of water in my face. "You son of a bitch," I yelled.

I woke to Carol Bergen daubing my head in gentle circles with a wet washcloth. Her brown eyes were concentrated and nurturing. "Don't talk like that," she said.

"I was talking to my suit," I said.

She looked at my suit. "I see what you mean," she said.

"Not this one. The one in my dream. It was… Forget it. It's not important."

"Doesn't sound it."

I reached for my neck, but she swatted my hand away. Carol handed me a bottle of whiskey that was nestled into the sofa-cushions between us and I took a long cool sip and let the liquor ooze onto my lap. She grabbed the bottle away.

"Don't touch it," she said. "I just wrapped it. It isn't so bad, but you'll have a pretty fever for a while, and you might think your head is going to fall off. But that's probably a familiar sensation."

Carol's free hand was glued to a glass of bourbon floated with ice. "I hate to mention it right now," she said, "but I told you about her."

"You didn't tell me everything."

"I didn't know everything." She folded the compress in halves and continued to dampen my skin.

"Let me have some more of that bottle?" I said.

"Be quiet and don't move," she said.

Dot came into the living room trailing an anemic doll. She sat down cross-legged next to her mother on the floor. The kid stared at me uncomprehendingly, exactly the same way I would have looked at me if I were a child.

"Did Ben smoke?" I asked. The words echoed around in my head as though emitting from a soundproof chamber, like I might have been communicating in rebuses.

"Never," she said.

I closed my eyes and grinned inwardly, but the grin slipped onto my lips and the tightening brought a wave of discomfort.

"There's something," Carol said.

"It isn't anything." I took the bottle from its perch, brushed it lovingly on my cheek to soothe the heat emanating from my wound. Then I downed the booze and handed the bottle back.

"I thought you didn't drink," she said.

"I don't unless there's some occasion."

"This is no occasion."

"I didn't say it had to be a good occasion."

"You're funny, Mr. Jome."

"I'm a few good laughs." I sat up. The soreness howled at me, then diminished somewhat. I couldn't move my head side to side—every swallow was like being crucified on bamboo. The room hadn't transformed. Still no pictures. Except for the orchard drawing.

"Where did all these awful things come from?" I asked, gazing at the drawing. "They're all over town, for chrissakes."

"Ben did them," Carol said. "When he was at the orchard."

"Why?" I asked.

"Why?" she asked back.

Mrs. Bergen shuffled off to the kitchen with the bottle. The kid was leaning forward and searching my face for some token of understanding, then quickly giving up. For such youth, she had a tired gaze inherited from her mother and a worn expression that had not evaporated from her face since I got there.

"So, it's not so bad after all?" I asked the kid.

She shook her head shyly, No.

Carol solemnly handed me a glass she'd brought back with her. When she instructed Dot to leave the room the child did so obediently.

"I thought a glass would make you more glamorous," she said.

I drank loudly, slurping and choking down the booze and the booze was gentle and good.

"Why don't you fetch the police?" she said in a concerto of ice-chewing. She was beside me on the couch, legs twisted under her.

"The police are too predisposed toward me at the moment."

She blinked, lowered a glance into her drink and lapped it back. I skipped the part about the two dead investigators.

"Besides," I said. "What are the police going to do when I tell them what happened? A crazy girl tries to murder me in her sleep."

Carol's eyes burned. "She was with you like that?" she asked.

I ignored her. "There's nothing that can be done. But I was paid and I intend to see it through."

"She's dangerous and you're lucky. There were many times…"

"Many times what?"

"She's just dangerous."

"She likes to think she is."

"She hated Ben. She hates me."

"Why's that?"

Carol shrugged and took the drink out of my hand and drank it. "Some people just hate. I can't remember if I hated her first or not. It doesn't have to make any sense."

We shared a drink, watching the day tumble in through the window like old substantial friends who have not had a conversation in weeks. Between lovers silence can be an eloquent description of contentment; but between everyone else it's usually just awkward. I was getting to enjoy Carol's company and I didn't want to enjoy it.

The creases in her tight expression cracked apart as her mind wandered. She shivered at something. The quiet was munching on the both of us. I put the glass on the coffeetable.

"You're good," she finally said, putting a hand on my arm.

"I'm not too good," I said.

"I think you're better than most."

"That's because most are awful."

"It was a compliment." The liquor was starting to depress her. "Why did you ask about that smoking thing?" she said.

"Nothing much," I said. "Just something."

"What kind of something?"

"The kind that might be nothing."

Suddenly Dot trudged back into the room hugging a blanket. Now I could see that she was a severely nervous kid who would grow up to be a severely nervous woman. Big round eyes of chalky blue. Experts whose job it is to reveal the sorrow of everything say that the older a person gets the more squinted their eyes become. Because the flesh around them expands, they say. The person is slowly shutting the world out of their world. And Dot was almost at that fine line when you stop wondering how birds can remain in a perfect V and you start wondering why your husband doesn't watch you anymore when you're removing your stockings or where your next paycheck is going to come from.

I looked at Dot and had miserable thoughts.

Quietly, Carol called her over and plunked her down in her lap. Dot didn't move or say anything. One of Carol's heels slipped off, displaying a sloppily painted set of pink toenails, feet excessively dainty. And I don't know why, but I was suddenly clear.

"When was it that Ben died?" I asked her, enunciating each word.

She considered while making a face that seemed to question my intelligence.

"Two years ago," she said.

I stood quickly. "Why didn't you tell me that?"

"Tell you what?"

"What you just told me."

"You didn't ask. Why would I think you didn't know that?"

The phone's ringing pounced in my ears and I believed for a second that it was my own anger.

"I got to go anyway," I said.

"Where?" she asked.

"Up to the orchard," I said. "I'm tired of this but if I don't do something I won't be able to do anything. Whatever it is, it's there."

It was trite and meaningless, but now that I knew why it was so trite and so meaningless it was neither and I couldn't really specify what it was, except to say that I was exhausted and that my neck was sore.

Carol let me borrow the bottle for the night when I left her place. Cold and achy, I was also febrile and on the verge of being totally delusional. I'd refused Carol's offer to call a taxi service. To steel myself for the trek to my apartment I drank tiny gulps from the bottle.

Cold wind numbed the gash. The street everywhere was coming reluctantly into summer, albeit with the torrential rain diligently constant. Directly ahead of me a lone, brown-uniformed garbage collector hurled a bag into the jaws of a leisurely idling truck. I resumed walking and Wald stepped from behind the truck. And from around the corner Lewishom appeared in a phone booth, not saying anything into the receiver. Leo was getting the works in a barbershop window down the block. Behind me the Ford crept along, going ridiculously slow to keep me in sight. I continued drinking and watching all these people gathering into this dark comedy.

All these people, and what the hell for?

Darkness was already getting close at 4:30. Over to the east through a crook in the sepulchral buildings the river was just a sound that carried meekly. Streetlights were snapping on, threw crooked lights onto the pavement. A woman with stringy hair propositioned me in front of the county clerk's office. I shook my head. Looking back after her I saw that she was not there, recollected her face as the face of one of my ex-wives. Sure, I was demented.

At 12th Street I leaned against a statue of a city founder that had been erected before the city he founded realized he'd embezzled thousands and had drunk himself to death in one of those stories that keeps getting retold. The same stringy-haired prostitute came back and inquired again if I might like to have a lot of fun. I dug my hands into my pockets and walked on. She trudged alongside me for three blocks and receded off with the other phantoms that stalk a man at his lowest.

It took me two hours and 30 minutes to go 30 blocks, regularly a 40-minute jaunt. Where had I been? Walking had become another dream, along with the city, the past and the Longtrees. I buried myself in the bed. Of course I did not sleep. An hour later I was up.

I boiled three eggs and for minutes I watched them crack and bubble up to the surface. I was jittery, on the border of becoming completely anxious, and my neck ached bad. I was still drinking, but the liquor had ceased working.

Of all people it was Richard Longtree who called to give me the news.

An hour earlier Sue Longtree slid into a relaxing bath with a hairdryer, wearing a shower cap, etcetera. The hairdryer was plugged into a socket and the shower cap was a mystery.

"What was she wearing a shower cap for if she was planning to kill herself?"

"I didn't inquire."

"Why are you calling me, Richard?"

"Because I'd like to talk to you."

"Is that a threat?"

"You were employed by her," he said sourly.

"I know. That was my third mistake."

"And I'd like to show you something and maybe you can figure it out."

"Drop by the office sometime. If you're hungry I have a few extra hardboiled eggs."

"Thank you, but I am not hungry. Come by my hotel. The Melancthon. I'll be the one in the lobby grieving."

The fact that Sue was dead sunk in when I put the phone down. Too bad. I liked her and her red hair. I liked her red hair a lot. But at the moment I was too transfixed by my own grief to weep. Women like her are exquisitely tuned to self-annihilate at a definable point. You don't have to know when it will be. Just that it will be big and loud. Why I wasn't able to feel anything for a woman I'd slept with so recently was the real dilemma. I honestly hated her.

I had some more whiskey, emptied out the bottle and stumbled around in the kitchen.

I thought a bit about Sue as the windows cried rain, shucking the eggs and eating them out of the pan.

I stared at the moist yellow yolk in a bitten egg.

Then at the turgid sky.

And back at the egg.

Absolutely no connection.

I threw on a raincoat.

Cowper and a bland-looking uniformed officer were sitting in the hallway on two folding chairs they must have requisitioned.

"You bring those chairs with you for the stake-out?" I asked.

"You have egg on your face," Cowper said in his weary voice. Even his suit looked bored. Bored and wrinkled. And clean.

"Why didn't you just knock on my door."

"We wanted to surprise you, Jome. And you having egg on your face is not an expression. There's egg on your face."

I wiped the egg away.

"Did Sue leave a note?" I asked.

"Aren't we investigating you?" Cowper asked. His ever-present bent cigarette was held behind his ear.

"She leave a note or not?"

"You're kind of forward, aren't you?" the officer asked.

"Progress tends to go that way."

"There was a note," Cowper said, shooting the officer a look.

"What did it say, if you don't mind."

"It didn't say anything, and I do mind. Left on the edge of the tub and the water erased the ink." Cowper paused, glancing back at the officer scornfully. "There's something not quite right about anything," Cowper said. "Why am I thinking that?" he directed at me. "I'm not sure why I'm filling you in, but I suppose it's because I'm soft. Would you like to explain any of it? Weren't you with her this afternoon?"

"Where'd you get that?" I asked.

"I asked."

"I'm cursed," I said, opening my arms wide. "Both my mother and father died during my birth. A few distant cousins, too."

"You should have been a fucking colonel," the officer said, and Cowper looked at him like he was going to bite him.

"Yeah," I said. "Or a little compelling."

Cowper lifted his small frame off the chair and then picked up the chair. The officer followed suit, none too pleased by the movement.

"What are we going to do now?" the officer asked Cowper.

"Just shut up," Cowper said. "Some people would like to know," he said to me, "what you've been doing in the Longtree business. By some people, I mean me. And by business I don't mean business. How about a chat?"

"I don't think I have the time right now. I'm going to meet an idiot."

"Did I mention that the Longtree broad's hands were tied behind her with her own bra?"

"The woman was indescribable and it wasn't beyond her to tie herself up. And no, you didn't mention that."

"You don't really care about her, do you?"

"I never claimed to."

They carried their chairs behind me and down the stairs and gaped at me from the front steps as I hailed a cab.

The effeminate bandleader was mopping his brow in the hotel lobby, hand resting on a Persian rug draped over the back of a plush couch. Around him frightened bellhops, eager for tips, bustled like billiard balls on a hustler's table. Wealthy vacationers chatted nearby about how much money they had. Dark red was the theme of the Melancthon Hotel and there were no variations on that repetitive motif.

Richard was wearing a wrinkled tuxedo that did his short stature and shining head no favors. His bowtie was completely upended, as though it were threatening him.

"Well, Jome, here we are," he said, rising lugubriously. "Just two jerks in a motel lobby somewhere."

"Good introduction," I said. "Is there anything else on your mind?"

"How's my dead wife doing?"

"Have a seat, Richard. You're going to get upset."

"Did you get what I just said?"

"Yeah. And I replied that you should sit down probably."

"It isn't easy to sit down at a time like this."

"Try it. Sit down, Richard."

He straightened his bowtie without any improvement and plunked back onto the couch. "OK," he said. "I'm sitting."

I lowered myself beside him and crossed my legs. Drawn deeply into the tux Richard looked like he was striving to spontaneously combust. "You look bad," he said.

"I feel bad. Last time I slept was for a few moments right after your wife tried to kill me."

There was no surprise in him. "Why'd she do that?"

"She didn't mean to. I was just handy."

"I should feel something, shouldn't I?" he asked himself, then answered: "But I don't. I'm too lazy to have emotions of any kind."

"Are you going to tell me you loved her or something?"

"If by love you mean I liked to see her suffer, then yes, I did love her."

People were stomping out of the lobby for an evening stroll or a dinner engagement. Whenever the revolving doors moved you could hear a blast of hammering rain. The guy I knew as Sid Lewishom entered the lobby in his blue sweater and corduroy pants, saw me and blushed. Immediately he sequestered himself in one of the phone booths.

"What day is this?" Richard asked.

I thought and I couldn't think. "I don't know."

"Neither do I." he said. "But here's something interesting and really honest. I loved her money. And her a little bit. Wow, I'm not sure what that makes me."

"It makes you, you. What money?" I asked. "I thought she was buying fruit with your money?"

Richard laughed a cheeky laugh, separated his lips to say something and let them flap open without talking. I hated him for his weakness and for everything his wife had represented.

"I think I did love her," he said. "Can I show you something, Jome?" Richard held out his hand like he was going to escort me to a dance.

"Some etchings?" I asked, getting to my feet.

We rode the elevator to the ninth floor. Neither of us spoke. Smells of cleaning chemicals, deodorizers, wet laundry and Richard's eau de cologne hugged the air inside his suite. He showed me the bathroom first. A tub full of water.

"I was in the tub when the call came that she'd drowned," Richard said. "I can't bring myself to drain it. Isn't that funny?"

"It depends on what you think is funny."

"I suppose it does," he said. "I have never appreciated irony as I should."

On the desk by the curtained window there was a stack of records on a portable record player and a carton of cigarettes and some keys. Then I noticed the serpentine woman on the bed. She was tall and fair-skinned, with explosive blue eyes and legs that could have touched the bottom of the ocean.

"Who's she?" I asked.

Richard squatted down beside her and ran a hand through the girl's auburn hair. "She's just a whore," Richard said.

"He likes to watch me have sex with myself," the girl said in a cute, sighing voice, the voice of a sweet girl trying too hard not to be a sweet girl. "I'm trying to be an actress and he says it's good practice to have people watch you doing embarrassing things."

"She's trying to be an actress," Richard explained. "And I did tell her that once or twice. She listens and she's a good girl. Aren't you a good girl?"

"I'm a pretty good girl," she agreed. Richard's small eyes shone when he stared at her.

He went to the sideboard and poured bourbon into two glasses and dangled one in front of me. His hands trembled and some of the bourbon splattered onto his black loafers. It was painful to swallow but I drank it down regardless. Richard lit a cigarette and wedged it in the ashtray he was carrying. Then absent-mindedly he lit another, set aside the ashtray, and loaded the second one into a fancy pearl holder.

"I may quit the music business," he said.

"That sounds like it would be to the advantage of the music business," the girl said and turned over on her side away from us.

"You're being rude," Richard said to the girl.

"You never let me leave this room. How am I going to become an actress if I can't leave this room?"

Richard smoked daintily, like a puppet would. He stared into his bourbon.

"So what is it?" I asked him.

"Just this. You asked about Sue's money. Where she got it."

"I remember."

"Have you ever encountered the name Dominic Early?"

I wasn't used to being surprised. "Constantly."

Richard puffed in a self-satisfied manner on his cigarette. The smoke was enveloping the room. The girl on the bed waved her arm to disperse the invasive clouds.

"Sue is Dominic Early," Richard said. "That must be worth something to you."

"It would be if I knew what you were talking about."

"Early is a pseudonym. Sue's a mystery writer. It's actually pretty bad stuff but people like pretty bad stuff and it sells well. That's why I hired those fools to tail you. Thought you and Sue were cavorting, if you know what I mean."

I set the glass down on the table.

"You've known this for a while?" I asked dumbly. "About Sue being Early?"

"Of course," he said. "I thought maybe I could use it

against her. There must be some money involved in the information."

Something shipwrecked inside me. In one motion I snatched the cigarette from his confused mouth and stuck it in my own, and as his eyes glazed over in stupidity I hauled back and caught him in the nose and heard a snap. Contorting for a soft place to fall, Richard tottered and I got him again and this time he brought the radio to the carpet with him, switching on a Beethoven sonata, one of the late ones that I especially adore. I pressed him deeper into the floor and I hit him in the back of the head, again, and then again, and he was limp under my weight so I hit him again, so rapidly it sounded like someone was urgently knocking on the door. And I hit him again.

I was breathing hard and he wasn't breathing at all. Setting him gingerly on the bed I saw that the girl was looking at me. I picked up the radio and brought it down on his head and the radio shut off. The girl wasn't afraid. She was turned toward me, frowning at Richard's crumpled head.

"Richard?" she said. Noticing that he wasn't going to be getting up again, she swept the hair out of her eyes and said, "Are you a producer or something?"

"Sort of, yeah," I said. "What's your name?"

"Gwenn," she said.

"Gwenn what?"

"Just Gwenn."

"I'm sorry you had to be here."

"I'm sorry wherever I have to be. But I've seen worse, so don't expect me to be shocked." She got off the bed wrapped in a transparent sheet and slipped on underwear with the sheet still around her. I watched, transfixed by her slim, senseless body. I was thinking of Sue, but not too much. "If you knew how much worse I've seen you'd be sorry for believing I feel bad about this."

"You look good," I said.

"I have to," she said.

"How long have you been here?"

"Couple of days. Five, I think."

"Did you like him?" I asked.

"Who?"

"The man on the floor."

"He was OK," she said. There were bruises on her back

and some on her arms.

I told her to finish getting dressed and she went into the bathroom with a bundle of clothes. After five minutes of watching him intently, I was confident that Richard was dead. My fever was back. I poured another glass of bourbon and swallowed it fast.

The girl reappeared in a light blue dress with white polka-dots, hair pulled back with a clasp, black heels that displayed her hardened calf muscles. Clothed, holding onto a white purse, she had the bearing of a depleted wife. Pretty, but not so pretty as to be annoying. I liked her instantly.

"This was a good meet—cute," she said.

"I guess," I said.

"Thanks for what you did," she said.

I nodded and she nodded back.

It was too soon to feel anything other than an escalating calm that nudged me light-headed to the elevator, the girl clasping my arm. A porter was reading some financial reports inside and he was doing his best not to notice me or the girl and maneuvered the buttons without looking up.

In the lobby I turned to the girl, who looked odd and satisfied. "You have a place?" I asked.

"I'll find one," she said.

I left her in the lobby.

Since Cowper had appropriated my gun I swung by my pawnshop and picked out a nice .38. When I asked for bullets the Hungarian said the gun had been brought in loaded and that if I needed more I was likely planning something and he couldn't, morally, sell me the piece. I told him six would be fine and he stuffed the gun in a paper bag.

I **didn't pack anything** except for the pistol. Before I left I called Cramm to yell at him. The suit wasn't ready yet. I went down to the parking garage below my building—the kind of place you have to sneak into to retrieve your car. Some trivial gangland characters in torn leather jackets were exchanging money and handshakes and ignored me.

The antique Buick was dark blue, highlighted with patterns of rust. I sank in behind the wheel and the engine woke all right. I wanted a quiet drive; sadly the radio wouldn't shut off, and only tuned to a big band station. I blew a layer of dust off the dashboard and put the heap in reverse. Getting to Sutter Falls would take about seven hours. Now it was just hitting on 10:30 a.m. on a plain Monday, maybe Tuesday.

The morning was chilly and alien. I'd rarely left the city to fend for itself, and I worried about it for a minute. Outside of the sprawl there were hardscrabble houses buried in junk and mounds of wheels and general debris. An hour after I left the rain snapped off. I was dozing and swerving off the dirt shoulder of the back road, windshield wipers waving extraneously. I stuck my hand out the window and cranked the radio, some over-the-top Benny Goodman stuff. Gearing onto the highway the world abruptly changed from coarse gray to brilliant gray. There were trees and grass and other surprises like those. Hills tapered off into valleys, valleys into mountains. Without warning the sky was suddenly bluer than I had ever seen it.

Sometime before five I was passing the billboard: SUTTER FALLS WELCOMES AMERICA, set in furious yellow print, as though the invitation hadn't been reciprocated.

The hamlet was clenched in a hushed valley. Distant church steeples pointed at an innocent sky and competed with the exorbitant number of water towers. Even in advance of reaching town I felt a languor you could have sprinkled on cold chowder.

Behind me a green sedan slowed when I did. I couldn't

remember whether it had been there since I deserted the city. I was tired and paranoid, but especially I was tired. Soon, the green sedan wasn't behind me anymore.

The first establishment I met in Sutter Falls was a low bar with a dirt driveway and one pine tree, called The New Place. On its sign was an oversize moose, its tail mechanically wagging in neon. But the town's nucleus was a row of store-fronts evacuated of any buyers or any marketable charm. There was a clothier's that doubled, as if on second thought, as a grocer's, and a barbershop and another barbershop right beside the first barbershop.

No traffic even at that early hour, and the three stoplights in town were all blinking yellow. A family of five rocked in rocking chairs on a porch stoop, watching me as though I were the World Series. Farther down, a black dog wandered into the street.

The difference between Sutter Falls and a ghost town was a flimsy interpretation.

My motel seemed to be the only one around, wedged in between the bus depot and an ambiguous stone structure that was either what the local masons did for a joke or some site of dubious worship. In comparison, the tawdry glitter of the motel looked to have been dropped there on a flight to Atlantic City.

The Belgian manager was glaring angrily at a pornographic magazine as if the model was his daughter's best friend. Long gray hairs sprouted from the unbuttoned parts of his print shirt. Underneath the desk he grappled for a second and I heard the sound of a zipper, standing at the same moment as his pants were pulled up and belted.

"Room?" he asked skeptically. He was broad and appeared to be either slightly dumb or very smart. His gray-ing mustache drooped as though it were wilting. One huge ringed finger employed the hunt-and-peck method on a clip-board clamped with sign-in forms. From the pocket of his tan wool cardigan he produced a cheap ballpoint pen.

"We had a conversation," I said. "I need the room that William Florence stayed in."

"I recall explicitly our talk." He tended to his mustache while he unhooked a key from a little peg. I handed him some twenties.

"Sixteen," he said, "will be your room. My favorite number. One night?"

"Hopefully."

From somewhere behind him I could hear female giggling. He smiled at me deviously.

The staircase was a black crisscross of lines and railings. I wasn't exactly sure why number 16 would be on the third floor. I heard footsteps above me, but when I halted the footsteps did too.

Room 16 was stuffy and cruelly decorated. A big rectangular reproduction of an 18th century fox hunt hung behind the bed, its lowermost frame hidden by the headboard. Someone had obviously gone through a lot of trouble to scour Sutter Falls for misused furniture and unload it fast. A rickety white card table was unfolded and circled with coffee-cup stains. Out the window there was a clear view of the bus depot and one person waiting there. I snapped the curtains shut. Somebody had left his dark suit in the closet. I tried on the coat but the shoulders pinched me.

Random filaments lined the bedside drawers: a Gideon Bible, unfinished scraps of love letters, a black, balled-up sock, one bottle of antacid tablets and a green, hardened slice of white bread. The telephone and the radio were chained to the lamp and neither worked.

I tried lying in the bed without touching the bed. One of the pillows had the scent of having been used as a hobo's death shroud. I closed my eyes and suddenly sprang up to see that I had been asleep for less than two minutes.

Around seven I unwound the bandage in the bathroom and soaked it in the sink and wrapped it back on. The mirror was grimed with what appeared to be an erased message written in lipstick. Bergen might have studied himself in the mirror before hefting the certainty of a fully loaded gun.

Pacing the terrible room I leafed through the Bible, that first, monstrous piece of detective fiction. Those dead prophets were all trying to uncover the biggest clue, and when he couldn't be found anywhere they imagined him everywhere for the sake of simplicity. I lifted the painting off the wall and traced the cloudy, badly painted splotch beneath it that was the end of Bergen and his promising golfing career. I stayed in bed for half an hour, listening to the pipes of the motel and the craven whisperings of an emptiness that wrapped tightly around me.

How long had it been since I'd slept properly?

I needed a drink so bad my hands were going clammy.

Down by the front desk the sounds of heavy intercourse were a zoological event. Walking to the bar I'd driven by earlier I was aware of someone behind me, as though the person were wearing metal-bottomed shoes and was proud to be in them. Every time I doubled back I spotted no one.

The New Place was well abandoned when I got there. At the far end of the bar there was a tall man with a red beard. His fancy cowboy boots were next to his stool. I sat at the bar and after five minutes the barman toweled off the counter in front of me and I ordered a coffee with a little whiskey thrown in.

"Really?" he asked.

I nodded.

Off in a corner Leo was playing his guitar very low, just brushing the strings like he didn't want anyone else to overhear, gently tapping his foot to get the rhythm right. After a few moments a couple of tall fellows showed and set up drums and an upright bass and started to fool around with Leo's melody. The small guitarist glared at the men, stuck his guitar in a black case and hopped onto a stool near me and pouted. He started haggling with the barman about the prices and wouldn't relent until the barman started mixing my drink. Then Leo apologized.

"Get out of this town," Leo told me. "I'm telling you."

"Shut up," I said.

"Huh?" the barman said.

"Nothing," I said.

Leo chuckled and took his guitar case out into the night.

Bringing me the concoction, the barman said, "This looks a little harsh. Our coffee is terrible and our hard liquor warps wood."

"I'm feeling a little harsh tonight."

"You're entitled to your feelings." The barman was a short guy in a sailor's white coat. "That everything for you?"

"Should be," I said.

"Glad to hear it."

"Glad to say it."

When he turned I asked what he knew about Daddy Longtree, and he shrugged helplessly.

"He came in here a while ago often enough. The Longtrees

are the Vanderbilts of Sutter."

"Recently?"

"Yeah. Two or three weeks ago, I guess."

"And what did you hear?"

"That he wasn't too social."

"What'd he come in here for?"

"To drink with another guy."

"When was that?"

He slung the towel over his shoulder. "You seem interested," he said.

"I'm only pretending."

"Longtree is a weird one."

"Why do you say that?"

"He acts funny. He wouldn't drink his beer when the man he was with bought him one. He wanted hard cider and we don't sell hard cider so he didn't drink anything."

"What man?"

"Somebody I never saw before."

The barman started scrubbing the counter with a blackened cloth. I ate a handful of stale pretzels from a paper bowl.

"Why're you asking?" he asked.

"I was hoping you'd tell me."

He mopped the counter some more.

"He just acts funny," he said. "I know because he used to come in here all the time. Lately he's just a stranger."

The bearded man at the end of the bar moaned.

"You know anything about his son?" I asked.

"Ben Longtree?" The barman nodded, solemnly. "Not much. Poor guy. Finished himself, I guess."

"How about William Florence?"

The barman contemplated. "William Florence sounds like a name I should know."

"But you don't."

"Yeah, but I don't."

I reached in my pocket and clawed out $35 and put it down. He stuffed the money in his own pocket. "I've still never heard of William Florence," he said.

"What'd the guy look like that Longtree was meeting?"

"Tallish, dark hair, I think. He wore a watch fob, I remember, and looked queer."

Refilling my glass, the barman said, "I don't know what it

was about."

"Could you guess?"

"Why would I guess?"

"Because I need to know."

"All I can tell you is that Longtree left in the middle of the conversation. Looked miffed. Guy stayed in here a minute, then he left too."

The door to the place swung out and Lewishom poked his large head in, saw me and poked his head back out.

"Thanks," I said.

"Yeah, thanks," the barman said back to me.

I drank the rest of my drink and hurried out.

Wald, the omnipresent guy in denim, was across the tree-lined intersection on the opposite corner, where an apartment building was unlit except for a man in an upstairs window examining his fingernails. I ran and caught up with the goateed man and grabbed his arm. He didn't resist. Behind us a clothing store shed bits of light.

For about two minutes we stared at each other. The shopfront was crammed with mannequins in various postures of abandonment.

"Call me Lewishom," the man said in a subdued voice. "Because that's my name."

"You already told me once. How about I don't call you anything until you tell me what you're doing around here?"

"I don't know what I'm doing."

"What do you think you're doing?"

Lewishom shrugged. The neckline of his blue sweater was frayed, and his gray hair was straight back. Out in the night there was nobody around. The sounds were mostly faraway predatory animals and the creaking of old buildings.

"Sue Longtree?" I asked.

He nodded again, sorrowfully, like he'd just divulged a paltry secret. "Look, Jome. I don't know what it is I'm supposed to be supposing. Just to follow you and keep tabs and that isn't a whole lot of much."

"Why?"

For the third time in less than a minute he bunched up his shoulders and gave me a doleful smile, lapsing into silence. A clock somewhere struck nine and when it stopped clanging I could hear a train rushing through the dark.

Lewishom was looking remotely at the mannequins,

pursing his lips and then licking them.

"The wife left me," he said, "and I've been in love with this unattractive burlesque dancer who doesn't know how much, or at all. I used to go by the club and watch her and act like she was dancing just for me. I thought maybe this gig would cheer me up, but it hasn't and it won't and I'll not get that girl."

Lewishom spit on the sidewalk and gazed at his saliva. "We're funny," he said. He was still shrugging every other second. "I don't know, Jome. Someone told me that everyone is like a carnival. You ever been to a carnival at two in the morning, when it's closed? It's the loneliest place on the earth. But I never really realized what that person meant until I went to a carnival. And even then I still didn't really get it." He shook his head. "I just don't know, Jome. I'm drunk on three-dollar gin so I'm not thinking too well."

"What are you going to tell me?" I asked.

"About what?"

"About anything."

He pointed at the window. "Those dummies have it made," he slobbered, and he turned unsteadily to a sedan parked beside us and got into the passenger seat. I started walking back to the motel, thinking he had nothing for me and was just one of Sue's extra men.

"Let me show you something," Lewishom said with his head craned out the window.

I stuck my hands in my pockets and dawdled over to his car.

"Just a sec," Lewishom said. He switched on the dome light, popped the glovebox. "Just let me see if I can—" and he rummaged through his junk and held something. It took me a second to see what he had, and then what he had glinted in a streetlight. The gun was a little snub-nose, too cheeky even for him. First he pointed it at his temple, next his chest and finally his forehead.

"Where are you supposed to do it?" he asked. "In the mouth, or what?"

"I don't think you're supposed to at all."

His elbow rested on the door frame, casually, like he was ordering a milkeshake at a drive-in. For about 20 seconds or 10 minutes we were busy being immobile. When I took my hands out of my pockets Lewishom scrutinized the movement. His gun wavered.

"Let me show you this," he said. "This is what it's like. OK?"

And the snub-nose rang out with a quick hollow echo. Lewishom flopped over the armrest, and the little gun clattered onto the pavement at my shoes.

"Hey," someone shouted. Above the clothier's the guy who'd been just a silhouette leaned halfway out his apartment window, beckoning. From his angle, I could imagine, Lewishom's farewell probably looked just a lot more insidious.

"I saw all of it," the guy screamed with a crack in his voice. Then he disappeared. Other apartments lit up.

I hurried through the dark, thinking how all of my acquaintances were shooting themselves, or jumping down staircases or sharing baths with appliances. I paused, fumbling for my keys. Inside, I paused again, leaning on the door. The sounds of a mild ruckus were out on the street. When I was done pausing for the night I ran a shower and just stood in it for an hour or two, my head rolling back on the porcelain tiles for momentary glimpses of rest.

I **was up all night** pacing the confines of my room. So far the whole thing was aimless. I'd accomplished nothing in the Longtree case except for driving my client to suicide, regaining my hankering for drink and managing to have been almost constantly awake for the past week. But I wouldn't be OK again unless this mess could be proven to have some kind of plot, a vindication for what precisely I thought I was doing. Real stories don't have morals or plots. My first misstep was thinking they did. Too much Dominic Early.

I puttered around the room for a few hours, conjuring any angle that would allow me to get out of Sutter Falls. It was no use. I had to push through with Daddy Longtree and the orchard.

Down in the lobby the next afternoon I had a black coffee in a cracked mug. I pressed the bell, glancing at the yawning ledger that had been opened on the front desk. My signature was second from the bottom, and facing it on the adjacent page was that of W. Florence in tidy, feminine cursive.

The Belgian manager came out of a backroom. Two female voices were berating him with foreign vitriol. A weariness had settled all over the guy and I was a little sad for him. He closed the door quickly, stood facing it pitifully for a moment, and came over.

"Know where I can get some apples?" I asked.

"Is that truthfully what you have called me out here in order for?" He pulled an unkind face. "Did you not hear those women?"

"Who are those women?"

"There's a grocery store three blocks down on Front Street. I'm sure they will have the apples you are looking for."

"Isn't there an orchard somewhere around here?"

"Longtree Orchard," he said, surreptitiously eyeing the backroom. "But it's nearly closed. The gift shop belonging to the orchard is straight for a half dozen miles and the orchard itself is a few more, I believe."

I put my room key on the counter. The Belgian turned and stared at a calendar tacked to the wall. February 9th had been circled and then crossed out severely and repeatedly. He hung the key with the other keys. Reluctantly he went back in with the women and I caught a better look at them: they were overweight, dark-haired twins blotched in too much eyeliner and wearing maid's gray smocks. They were frowning in tandem, ready to pounce. The Belgian watched me as he shut the door, his eyes pleading for assistance.

I had my own troubles.

Brisk lake air hit me in the eyes. The sun was out and it was an obnoxious glare after so long without a whiff of the bastard. Sweet blossom infused the wind, the torpor of childhood prowling about it. From the glovebox in my car I pulled a pair of dark glasses and strapped them on. Across the unlined road there was a restaurant with a dangling, hand-painted sign featuring a tottering farmer. I went in and had pancakes, an egg and three cups of black coffee.

For five miles I drove north under a forest canopy that shut out the sun. The gift shop was on the main road, a rustic log facade the size of a duplex. One of the triple garage doors was slightly lifted to reveal a gaping interior. Crates were stacked in the yard in disarray, and off to the side in a small pasture was a classic red pickup truck, tailgate rusted off, the tires flat. It was either the epitome of America or its thorough derision. The lake glimmered out of the high birch trees. Paddles muscled through the water, skiffs and speedboats dotting the shores.

But the shop was about as wholesome as lice.

I noticed a set of initials carved in the butt of a log in the front yard, bearing a time and the date, February 9th, below.

The orchard was a sprawling, tangled expanse of neglected trees clutching at brown apples. A broken fence spanned the grounds, rooted by posts nailed with paper arrows pointing up.

The shop's single, rustic room was decorated in framed awards from a dozen years back and canisters of spent pesticides. Little packets of seeds and wood chips were scattered across the floor. There were decomposed apples everywhere.

A young man with bristles of black hair sat on a stool behind the metal counter. He was wearing gold sunglasses and I couldn't tell if he was asleep or just lazy. The frazzling white light of a vintage television set flashed around him, but he was not looking at it.

"Guess who?" I asked loudly.

He didn't move and his soft face was inflexible.

"Is your Daddy home?" I asked.

"Daddy's always home, motherfucker. You know," he said warmly, "you remind me of someone I wouldn't like."

"There's more of me back in the car."

"You look tired as hell, pal. Maybe you just need to get some sleep and everything will be fine." The kid slouched forward and licked the paper of a marijuana cigarette he'd apparently been saving.

"So?" I asked.

"What happened to your neck?"

"I'm starting a fashion trend."

"It looks awfully terrible."

"They all do in the beginning. Where's Longtree?"

"He sold the place a week ago. It's not on the market."

"I'm not buying."

"It's going to become a retreat for wealthy, almost insane people."

"You're repeating yourself." He didn't get the joke and I wasn't sure there had been one. "Where is he?"

"At the cottage."

"Where's the cottage?"

"Far end of the dirt road."

"Where's the dirt road?"

He jerked his thumb over his shoulder. "Did you see that dirt road on your way up here?"

"Yeah."

"It's not that dirt road. It's another one."

"Which dirt road is it?"

"The other one." He lit the joint with a match and the flame sputtered in the lenses of his shades.

"It's the dirt road going north. But you'll have a hell of a time getting up there. We'll be out of here in a week, so you better get your business done fast."

"Sorry to hear that."

"Why're you sorry?"

"These days I'm sorry about everything I hear."

"You must hear a lot."

"Not nearly enough. I appreciate all the work you've put

into this," I said. I handed him a crumpled five dollar bill. "A little something for your trouble."

"Thanks, but I'm not going to thank you."

"You're welcome and you just did."

"I didn't mean it," he said. "Sorry."

I took a peek at the TV—nothing but static.

Back in the car I drove underneath a ratty wooden sign that had been eaten away and over a gradual incline of jutting boulders and hidden dips in the path. Dirt lanes ran the length of the orchard, intersecting, abruptly dead-ending, traversing the hills. All leading seemingly nowhere but up. I chose one at random. Liquefying apples popped under my tires, spraying sickening geysers at the windshield. Even with the windows down the vinegary smell of rot was pervasive.

Finally, I pulled up in the mud outside the cottage. Trees had collapsed all around the square pasteboard building, badly-fitted planks covering holes where windows should have been, hints of light glimmering in the cracks. The grass was four feet high except in those spots where some heavy-farming implement had been abandoned. I wasn't sure why I was waiting for darkness to come. I was drained and tried closing my eyes, but I was too tired for rest. I was too tired for anything, especially this.

Night fell in sharp checkerboard dividends around the branches and squat hills. A playful moon and a timorous solitude made the orchard look quaint and innocent. I waited until the horizon lost its pink afterglow, the motor humming me back to childhood. I noticed streams of chimney exhaust blankly ascending into the gravelly sky above.

The orchard brought a feeling I had experienced at my worst moments. Maybe it was a metaphor, but I didn't think much of metaphors. Besides, the presence of death everywhere doesn't beg poetry to have much of an imagination. The orchard was a symbol in a drawing, and I was entering that place where symbol and reality were difficult to wrench apart.

I shut off the motor and got out, immediately breathing in the dread that seemed to have constructed the place. From somewhere near the main road I heard the acceleration of a vehicle, and perhaps the creak of a door opening and not closing. And I heard nothing else but my own footfalls crunching on dead leaves.

I let myself in to the cottage. The stench of dead fruit had me incapacitated for an instant. I felt at the grip of the pistol tucked into my waistband.

The space was nothing but a wasted accumulation of old tools and sacks full of spilling apples, a compact fusion of kitchen, living room and bedroom. Daddy Longtree blinked at me from behind a table that was really just a long door propped up by cinderblocks. A lantern in the middle of the makeshift table provided only enough light to find the lantern itself.

Longtree was eating an apple pie with a butter knife. "I heard you out there in your car for about an hour or so. Hope you aren't scared of me," he groaned. He had a strand of gray hair combed toward his eyebrows, slight gray stubble that rose high on his prominent cheekbones and close-set dark eyes that were like bubbles on the surface of a swamp.

"I was thinking of being afraid," I said. "But I decided against it. There's enough fear in you for the both of us."

"I'm not afraid of you. I just met you."

"Right now I'm a little afraid of me. And not to get on a tangent, but what's that kid's problem out there?"

"He's just mean. He's an orphan. Orphans can be mean."

I grabbed a chair by the sink and brought it over to face him. He munched contentedly on the spoiled, mold-green pie. Moving things rummaged in the crust.

"They're going to build a lunatic asylum on my land," Longtree said. "What should I think of that?"

"They won't have to look far for inhabitants."

Longtree smiled, then grew serious and smiled wider. "I've been thinking," he said.

"That doesn't sound hopeful."

"It isn't." He scooped a large helping, bending his head and using his free hand to scrape a rogue apple slice into his mouth. Something pried its way from between Longtree's lips and skittered away.

"We all of us," he said, "have one day to go back into the dirt. I'm getting a head start." He scraped what remained of his brown teeth with the butter knife. "It's around that time when I should ask who you are."

"Whoever I am doesn't matter."

"Are you selling something?" he asked.

"I'm not selling anything."

"Everybody is selling something."

"What are you selling, Longtree?"

He lifted his eyes to the ceiling and contemplated the tears in the plaster. "I honestly don't think I'm selling anything."

"Who were you with that night at the bar?" I asked.

"What night?"

"That night you were there. Was it Florence?" The overpowering stench of vinegar was becoming familiar and less noxious.

"Who?" Longtree asked coyly. "Who is that? *Florence*?"

I was beginning to doubt someone and it wasn't me. "What about Ben Bergen, your son."

"I don't have a son," he said.

I stared at him as he plunged back into the pie. "You think that's a good angle?"

He peeked at me above a scoop of pie. "I'm not being cagey. I did have a son. Now I don't have a son. He died off a few years ago."

"How?" I blurted.

Longtree only shook his head. Frustration was getting a claw in me. I pulled the pistol out of my pants and put it on my lap.

"And what about your daughter?"

"I do have one of those. Sue. She's a belligerent girl. Sue has problems. It is a Longtree trait."

"Sue's dead too. Drowned herself in a tub."

Longtree had nothing in his face. "I sort of supposed that," he said.

"William Florence?" I said. "And I'm not really kidding. Who is he?"

"Yes, Will is an insurance man. He was digging in the Longtree family—something about a policy taken out on Sue by her sleazy husband. It's possible that he discovered more about the Longtrees than anyone ever had and was planning something. He was coming here to grease his hands. Which is probably what you're here to do as well."

"Ever read the papers?"

"No."

"I think Florence was the guy in the motel with the bullet in the back of his head."

"Does that concern me?"

"That depends on whether it concerns you. So Florence got

something on you and you paid him."

"I didn't pay him."

"What did you do?"

Longtree breathed and his breath was stale and wretched. "I didn't do anything."

"Somebody did something."

Longtree reached under the table and I tensed. The object in his hand was a book and he set it down between us. One apple-encrusted thumbprint was visible on the cover. He sighed. I looked at the flap: *A History of Death*. By Dominic Early. Of all people.

He said, "It's loosely based on the history of my horrific family, which you might know something about. All the names are changed, obviously, but it's a thrilling work. My father was a murderer, as was his father, and his father, et cetera, et cetera." Longtree belched. "There's no reason in it. Just inheritance of very bad genes, I guess. Every Longtree is a monster. You should be careful, Mr. Jome. They say that whoever struggles with monsters is likely to become one."

"Who says that?"

"My dead wife, actually. That's why I'm alone up here. I like being alone up here."

I crushed a beetle that was climbing up my pants leg and said nothing because there was nothing to say.

"I am the commonest man," Longtree said. "Aren't I? Wouldn't you say that I am the commonest man?"

I put the gun on the table and pointed it at him.

"Sure," I breathed. I couldn't stand his frazzled smirk any longer. Longtree only cut another dollop of bug-infested pie and pretended that the gun and I weren't there. Finished, he bent over and took something off the floor and handed it to me. It was the drawing of the orchard, although in this one the charcoal had been scratched off in places.

"That's the original," Longtree said. "I'd like it if you had it. I used to give copies of it to people I respected."

He paused and licked crumbs out of his facial hair with a wide tongue, laying the drawing on the table.

"I'm glad you're here though," he said. "Just to remind me why I'm here." He gazed longingly at the pie. "I am awfully glad you're here. I made the discovery long ago," as though reciting from a fairy tale, without pausing, "that I was a murderer. What made me kill Ben? I had no option. He told me how hard it was for him to function without the urge to kill someone. I don't think he ever did. But before I stopped telling him it was going to be OK my hands were around his neck and I had no control at all and he just let me do it." Longtree stared off calmly. "When he was dead I hung him in his garage. First time I'd been away from here. Everybody was sad for me. I was sad for me. Even now I don't have any guilt or anything. I wonder why that is?"

I slumped back in my chair. He continued to sputter on as he ate.

"I couldn't have anyone suffer. Ben was going to be a murderer like the whole course of his ancestry and I had to prevent that. And then I did prevent that. I was thinking of his little girl. I was also thinking of everybody else too."

Now he didn't use his utensil but just dug into the pie with his hands and stuffed a mound of apple and insects into his unperturbed grin.

"So now you are aware. You probably would have figured it out sooner or later," he said. "So how much do you want?"

I stared hard at Longtree.

"You know about farming?" he asked me, pricking up his eyes to meet mine. "First you have to care for each tree like it was a part of your own body. That's why my orchard is so successful," he said. "I got 50 pickers at least. I make such a nice apple pie. Mm-hmm." He tapped his ring finger twice on the pie tin. On the third tap his hands and his head dropped at the pistol's retort. I was mildly surprised that I had shot him. A billow of acrid smoke erupted to the rafters and stayed there. Longtree's legs twitched, kicking out an absurdly fast dance. He had one last breath to say something pithy, but it came out in a whisper that I couldn't hear and which smelled rankly of bitter almonds. I hadn't thought death would smell of bitter almonds. There were a lot of things I didn't know.

On my way out I had to laugh. Because of the Longtrees and my role in wiping nearly all of them out, directly or indirectly. Except for the daughter, Dot, who was the last of them. But she couldn't be a part of this grisly tale. My laughter fell flat in the cramped and anguished room, dying the split-second it pushed off my lips. Head turned to the ceiling, still seated at the table, Daddy Longtree was just a shadow—not anywhere near an imposing one, either.

For a minute I stared at the drawing of the orchard up close to the lantern, a hint of something important tugging at me, just off the border of the picture. What was it in the dark shapes and swirls that was I missing? My mind was all puckered, waiting. It seemed that it was all right there; the problem was that I couldn't be sure what "it" was supposed to be, "all" signified, or "there" was. The upturned furniture and the apples were starting to bother me, and so I folded the drawing and brought it with me. I imagined a voice coming from somewhere nearby, looked at Longtree, as inert as an ice sculpture.

The night was warm with the musty smell of imminent rain. Just outside in the grass I unfolded the drawing and peered at it some more. There was still something I was not getting but that was spelled out plainly in the charcoal smudges. Again I heard the muttering voice, the way someone might talk on the telephone from the other side of a thick wall, coming from a batch of tall trees to the east.

I waited with the drawing in my hands, not certain how to handle my delusions, if they were delusions. For the third time I wound the drawing into a tube and simply stood there listening.

Clouds had eaten the moon. Owls fluttered and sang, the trees soughed, animals moved about. It took a lot of effort not to think about anything. Underfoot the dirt crackled, and when I had my hand on the car door I heard something I shouldn't have heard, namely a man's voice starting to sing a lovely song and then instantly halting the lyrics.

"Jome?" the man said from the trees. "I was just thinking about you."

I swiveled, fearing for a second that the voice was my own and then fearing more that it wasn't.

"Jome," the person said again from a copse of trees surrounded by a clearing of fallen saplings.

"Who's asking?" I shouted.

"I am." The man's tone was high-pitched, recognizable, though I couldn't place the cadence, and possibly drunk. "I heard what you did. What'd you do anyway? In there with Longtree? You gone lunatic or something?"

I squinted through the twisted foliage, raising the pistol toward the sound. I couldn't make the man out.

"Longtree killed his son," I said. "So I killed him back. The story has a happy ending for everybody."

"Not for Longtree it doesn't."

Neither of us said anything for a minute.

"Which one are you?" I asked.

He said, "I'm Walt Wald."

"I figured."

"*Do* you have it figured, Jome? What do you think you're going to do now that you have it figured?"

"I haven't really gotten to that part yet. I was planning on getting in my car and driving back to the city."

"Tonight? That's a long drive. Maybe you should stay somewhere and start fresh in the morning."

"Are we talking about something, Wald? This has lost some track."

"Look, Jome. I'm a private investigator and Sue hired me to watch Lewishom and I just came upon him after you killed him in his car. Not very nice of you, Jome. I know what it probably looks like in Longtree's and I won't argue. But I thought you'd let me take you in because you're going to be in regardless and it would be nice if I could be the one to do it. That's two dead people. Knowing you I'm sure there's more squirreled away somewhere."

"Lewishom killed himself."

"That could be claimed about everybody in a way."

"That doesn't sound convincing."

"That Sue is a crazy bitch," he said. "Can you believe it?"

"She was," I said. I crouched low, aiming into the darkness. The moon was sneaking coyly out from the cluster of clouds now and when it did the clearing would be illuminated.

"Why the past tense, Jome?"

"She drowned herself," I said.

"When did she do that?"

"Earlier."

Ahead, the spot where the man was concealed was being slowly lighted.

"I just talked to her little while ago," the voice said. "That's too bad. How am I going to get the money she owes me?"

"I'm not sure, Wald."

"I'm not either. She told me she was going to Florida after all this."

And the moon flared, revealing the clearing and the tall, upright figure that was just a glancing silhouette and nothing more.

"What do you mean Florida?" I asked. "And what do you mean, all of this? What is *this?*"

"I mean," he started to say, and just then my gun interrupted him and the silhouette dropped hard with a scattering of twigs. I stood and got into the car. On the way back my headlights swept over the stoned kid from the office. He was wide-eyed and he was running for the cottage. I rolled the window down.

"Kid," I yelled at him. "It's a real mess up there."

His mouth said something and he kept running.

The strong breeze was invigorating and I was suddenly awake.

I returned through the wreckage of trees, all mold and utter sorrow. Nestled into a turnaround off the path a green sedan was parked, belonging, I guessed, to Wald.

I drove too fast, skidding into culverts and narrowly missing a few trees. Maybe I'd killed Longtree to offer some kind of resolution. Then again, I could have simply not known what to do. I blamed it on fatigue and confusion. But killing Wald couldn't be rationalized. Maybe it could.

Additionally, there seemed to be a gathering of private dicks out for me. Why had Sue hired all these people and had them follow me and each other? Nothing made sense.

Sue Longtree, I thought, probably deserved everything that she did to herself.

Why anything anymore.

And so Ben Bergen was what he'd always been: a name, and a face I'd never seen.

I was coming down with a rotten head cold, and endured a bout of sneezing while I drove.

I really wished the suit was done already.

Coming into view of Sutter Falls and back on paved roads I was overlooking the lake and the moonlight dinging off the surface. I braked and for five minutes I admired the water and the air, and then I felt stupid and kept driving. It was just past nine.

I passed fields and imagined lonely farmers on tractors inching through the fields.

I was sure that I was being followed, and a moment later I was sure I wasn't. Then I wasn't sure. Cars appeared and reappeared in my rear-view with inconstant regularity. I was convinced that both Wald and Lewishom were behind me somewhere in the night, still tenaciously on the case. I couldn't shake them. Every few miles I pulled off to the side. Twice I thought their respective cars had bypassed me when I was stopped. I learned to stop looking behind me.

The drawing was on the seat beside me and I repeatedly held it to the dome light, looking into the amateur lines for some kind of clarity. Finally I stuck it out the window and let the rush of wind have it.

The wipers were on the whole drive. Twenty minutes away from the city and it was pouring again. At each off-ramp into town I kept driving, until there were no more exits and there was just the highway.

Eventually I turned back. The city—the things and the places that were familiar and mine—suddenly felt somehow foreign.

At the office a legion of dust stalked the air and settled over the ruins of furniture. The reddish shadow from Parker's head had dulled to a milky relief, like the pigment you'd see in a Rothko.

Twelve minutes to 5 a.m. Sleeping would have been the right thing to do, but I was too exhausted and too haunted for the idea not to seem like a nightmare. Instead I stretched out under the window like a cat. Ants bustled on the wood near my face, and I felt like drowning some of them in my saliva. The gash in my throat was still bandaged and the sting had gone away but I could feel my heartbeat throbbing in the wound. I pried myself off the floor without any ants being harmed and gobbled a handful of aspirin. From a desk drawer I pulled a tissue, the cold now filling my head and eyes.

I was finished.

In a lunge of exotic dread I was suddenly emptying the contents of the filing cabinets one by one, yanking bygone cases and files and items from the drawers and just piling it all on the floor in a mania I couldn't explain but for an odd reason enjoyed. I blamed it on the Longtrees, along with everything else that was wrong.

After 20 minutes I'd tired myself out and sat and watched the city bounce around inside the room. The office was now a tangled mess of clutter, a broken mug scattered in the midst.

Maybe I was looking for something and by not finding it I was coming closer to realizing that there was nothing to find. The Longtree fiasco was itching me and I couldn't do anything about it. What had it been about?

I stood and tried to shake off my brain.

Rain smeared the windows and the lights outside. Then lightning flattered the night in an afternoon shine.

I smiled at the man in the window. He didn't smile back.

"What the hell is wrong with you?" I asked.

"I got a cold or something."

"That's too bad."

"Is it?"

And then I punched the window, but it didn't shatter and I tried again. Then I tried again and it still wouldn't shatter.

I looked at my knuckles. At the wall. At the dust. At the broken mug. Nothing felt right.

I was drifting off into a black-and-white dream when the call came in. I thought I recognized the soft-spoken, uneasy voice.

"Harry Jome?" the man asked.

"I think so. Let me check."

"Could you meet me right away? I'm at the diner near your building?" he said it like a question.

"I'm a little busy here just now."

"It's not unimportant. It's about Sue Longtree and some other things."

"I don't care about Sue."

"You might care about these other things," the man said and wasn't there. I pried myself into the elevator and got to the diner a minute later.

At a far booth inside the diner a skinny teenage couple were necking with every part of their bodies except for their necks. Both of them pimpled and as carefree as quantum physics. The place was drenched in artificial warmth. Behind the counter the waitress who'd caused the commotion a few days ago had returned to her job, obviously pregnant and obviously angry about it. The teenage boy glared at me as though I was his girl's uncle come to take her home.

The man at the counter was in a gray tweed suit and brown spats. He had a stoic profile. He was too poised and pale to belong there. His salt-and-pepper hair was long and parted and hadn't been touched by a barber in months. A mustache fit perfectly on his upper lip. His umbrella had fallen underneath his stool, and near his elbows there was a stack of stapled papers.

I wedged into the stool beside him and shook my head when the waitress asked me what I'd have.

"Jome, isn't it?" the man asked. When he turned his eyeballs were crystals, very blue and very careful.

"You Florence?" I asked back.

"No, but it's still nice to know you. Sorry about the circumstances."

"I don't know what the circumstances are."

He shrugged. A cup of coffee was pushed off to the side.

"Are you Florence?" I asked. "Or Bergen or some other asshole?"

"I should be somebody," he said, using his fingers to taper his mustache.

"Whoever you are you've caused a lot of stupid dying and I'm the one going to be chained up for it."

"People sometimes die," he said casually. "Isn't it better that it's for a reason?"

"What's better for a reason?"

"What I'm telling you."

"So far you haven't told me anything."

"I haven't?"

"No."

"I thought I had. Well, I'm saying that those deaths were kind of not my fault. By the way, how many people have you killed in the past couple of days?" His mustache twitched like it was trying to leap away from his mouth.

"OK. So I don't know what you have or if you have anything," I said. "Ben Bergen is dead but used another name and I can't track down Florence, which is the name he used. And Sue is dead and a couple of nerds called Parker and Porter," I realized that I was counting the dead on my fingers. "Lewishom. Wald, I think. Maybe even somebody I've never heard of."

The man nodded and bit both his lips at the same time.

"Maybe I'm the guy you've never heard of," he said. "Dean Bruckner. I have an office just below yours and it gets more silly in a second. We're in the same line of work."

"How did that happen?"

"The Longtree lady needed somebody good to follow you and the guys following you and to keep eyes on how it was going."

"I never noticed you."

"Because she needed somebody good. I just told you. And I'm a little proud of that."

"You shouldn't be."

"I am, though."

"So what?" I said. "What about Bergen and Florence."

"I don't know anything about them but I do know that neither of them has anything to do with this."

Bruckner's troubling eyes were mellow with the intensity of brooding over intense things. The light in the room was all crooked, like an origami construction of shadows.

"Ever hear the name Dominic Early?" Bruckner asked.

"I know all about Domoinic Early. He and Sue are the same person. A hack writer of juvenile stuff."

"I'm glad you know Early is Sue because that's the big explanation."

He slid the stack of pages over to me. I flipped the manuscript over. The title was big and blatant and contained five words: *The Last Orchard in America*. And below that, *A Novel by Dominic Early*.

"Jome, you were research for Sue's latest dumb potboiler and I was the researcher," Bruckner said. "She hired me to track you around town. She was all blocked up, she said. The case was only for a plot of hers. All she wanted to do was stir things up by hiring a bunch of investigators and see what popped out of the disorder."

"Is it any good?" I asked without knowing why I asked.

"She's not a good writer and it has no ending. It does include her suicide though. Maybe you can conclude it if you want to."

Somewhere within me everything halted. The answer I had was to the question I hadn't asked. I was so enraged I felt almost weightless.

"So what do you want?" I asked. "You and Sue got away with something. I was a character in her book. I'm not sure what she got away with, but something happened and you must have been causing something to happen. Or else you wouldn't be here with my phone number in your pocket. So what about Bergen? What about anybody? What the hell went on?"

"The answers are all there Jome. Your problem is that there are no questions."

"So what do you want, Bruckner?"

Looking at me, he puzzled over how he was going to phrase it. "I thought you should know about her manuscript," he finally said. "And I also wanted to tell you how bad of a private investigator you are."

He curled his lips into a rictus that didn't spread to the rest of his face.

Halfway out the door, yanking up his umbrella, he turned

and asked too pleasantly: "Is it ever going to stop raining?"

The horny couple was staring at me and they were frightened at what they saw. I followed Bruckner out to the drenched street. Lightning burned the sky a crimson blush.

It was never going to stop raining.

I had Sue's manuscript in my hands, and I raised it above me to shield off some of the downpour. I wasn't going anywhere, if I ever had been.

Another flash of lightning exposed Bruckner conferring with someone under an archway. I couldn't see who it was. I took a handkerchief out of my pocket and daubed my cheeks and forehead. I looked at the handkerchief and saw that it was moistened with wet gray ink. The manuscript's print was dripping all over me and I choked a little as it swept into my mouth.

No, it wasn't ever going to stop raining.

Standing there soaking on the stoop of the diner I imagined the oceans and the rivers and reservoirs outside of town that nourished the city all breaking loose and ripping apart and absorbing the brick facades and the embellished cornices and the stairwells and small sports cars and vending carts and street signs and deck chairs and expensive dresses. I realized that I hated everything that had ever been. Because it was not going to stop raining.

I conjured an image of my suit and the image wouldn't leave me. It was a flawless suit, and in my pondering it fit me better than my skin. I wanted to be in that suit.

I walked and walked and there were low voices all around me in the dark. Soon I was in front of my tailor's and my rage was ballooning. His basement shop was brightly lit. I let myself in through the front door and descended the stairs. The room was inhabited by five or six headless mannequins in various postures. Cramm had his back to me in a monogrammed bathrobe, his black hair disheveled.

"Where's my suit, Cramm?" I asked, startled by the ferocity in my voice.

He spun around and backed up into one of the mannequins, dropping a piece of chalk. One of the figures was wearing what I imagined my gray suit to look like, white lines running up and down the sleeves and pants.

"It looks pretty done to me," I said.

"Almost, sure," Cramm said, fear set in his eyes. After a

second he said, "The cuffs aren't sewn on yet."

I advanced toward him. "I don't give a damn about the cuffs. I never figured you to be this kind of person, Cramm. I'm disappointed."

"Sorry," he said. "But the suit is not done."

Cramm was shaking when I went by him and tilted my head at the suit. The fabric was satiny. I hadn't seen a better suit, even considering the white tracings. This suit was the sartorial version of a ballad.

The tailor was crying and going for the staircase slowly. I pulled the pistol and fired, and the shot caught him in the hip and he fell behind some cardboard boxes.

I lifted the three-piece job off the mannequin and stripped, putting the rain-blanked manuscript on a stool. Removed my pants and jacket and slipped into the smooth seersucker I'd been waiting for. The fit was grand. I took the manuscript and passed Cramm groping at the bottom stair.

"What's all this for?" he said.

"For not having my suit done faster."

"The cuffs still need to be measured," he said weakly, and then I think he died.

"I like it how it is," I said.

Soon I was under a streetlight and some men were scurrying around the dark buildings. I turned down an alleyway, glancing back to see some fellow entering Cramm's shop and gesturing for others.

I felt better with the suit on.

A sirocco wind had sprung up and the bridge swayed over the river, and the river smelled of beached fish and that peculiar pungency that water gives off before dawn. It was 5:39.

There was a barge somewhere off in the night. Foghorns throttled out every few seconds like a slow, dense clock. The bridge was empty of pedestrians and vehicles, the parapet below shaded by trees, the starless-ness of the sky jumpy with accumulating tempests.

"Wow," Leo said, and let out a sibilant noise. He had his forearms on the railing. He looked wearily out toward the harbor.

"Where's your guitar?" I asked.

"I gave it up. I'm no good at it."

"Sure you are," I said.

He perked up. "You think?"

"Sure."

"OK," he said, pushing off from the railing. "OK. And look, you got that suit. Maybe I'll get one."

"You really should," I said.

"I really might," he said, and he patted me on the shoulder and drifted off, whistling. He disappeared down the length of the illuminated parapet, and then the whistling stopped.

I put two hands on the metal supports and whistled Leo's tune. I hadn't whistled in a while. The resonance across the harbor was like some lost lullaby repeated from someone I'd never met. I whistled and whistled, a whistling maniac standing on a bridge. Wearing a fresh suit.

I held out my palms. It wasn't raining anymore. I was glad. I was so glad I upped the volume of my dirge.

And then I wasn't whistling anymore.

The same is true for the end of a story as it is for the beginning: where do you say it's finally done? At the moment all of the various stupid actions make fate inevitable? That moment could have been all along.

Endings are always the same because they're usually not the same.

Ink from Sue's book stung my eyes and bled down my face. It tasted rotten and the taste stayed. Below me, the river clashed with the pale banks, flooded onto the grass of a park. The night was everywhere, and even though the rain petered out, it still dripped from the intricate trusses overhead.

The ending could have been a batch of spotlights from the north side of the bridge, and the anomalous quietude of daylight shining through the darkness.

Could have been the silence of the men holding the spotlights steady and the displaced whispers of their supervisors.

Or Cowper, materializing out of the spotlight, the way you can tell by his posture that he's serious. Bent cigarette held in between his lips and looking as though he'd forgotten about it since last he'd visited me.

Any ending could be what he said to me on the bridge.

"Why'd you do it, Jome? All those people? Any reason whatsoever?"

Could have been my response, that maybe I was just frustrated with the whole goddamn idea. "I haven't slept too well lately," I said. "If only you understood how much of this I don't understand."

The end could have been the remnants of leftover rain slaloming off Cowper's hat or the men behind Cowper who were giving themselves shapes in the spotlight.

Suddenly I felt the great thrill of feeling nothing and the feeling was good. And that would have been a partly decent ending.

Cowper approached casually, as though we'd planned to meet here. Two of the men were close behind him. Now that I had my suit on I was ready, and it didn't matter that the suit wasn't finished. I pulled myself onto the bridge's railing, head lowered to the clamorous river.

The end could have been that I didn't care, or it could have been something as simple as a nod, because these kinds of things usually end on a bridge.

END

MORE FROM THE2NDHAND